REDEEMING THE BILLIONAIRE

THE SHERBROOKES OF NEWPORT

CHRISTINA TETREAULT

Digital ISBN: 978-0-9883089-9-2
Print ISBN: 978-0-9906511-0-9

For more information on the author and her works, please see www. christinatetreault.com.

ONE

TRENT GLANCED down at the Patek Philippe Aquanaut on his wrist. It was fifteen minutes until he was expected in his father's office; more than enough time to grab a cannoli from the bakery located near the courthouse. He didn't know what the bakers at Ambrosia did to their pastries, but their cannoli were the best he'd had anywhere.

Crossing the street, he pulled out his smartphone when it beeped letting him know he had a text message. *Another message from Lindsey.* He'd told her when he relocated to Rhode Island a month ago he had no idea when he might be back in London again. If all went as he hoped, he'd remain here in Providence until he made his way to the United States Senate. Without stopping, Trent typed out a message as he walked toward the bakery, the scent of the pastries and espresso already making his stomach rumble and he hadn't even stepped inside yet.

He hit an object and heard the startled cry of surprise seconds before the hot coffee splashed across his hand and phone. The message forgotten, he looked down at the living object he'd just run over. "I'm sorry about that. Are you okay?"

He knelt down to help the woman retrieve the papers she'd dropped. Several were covered with coffee, as was the front of her blouse.

"I'm fine." The woman stacked the pages together and stood. "I'll need to reprint these though." She accepted the pages he held out to her.

Trent stood and without a second thought, he reached into his suit jacket and pulled out a case holding his business cards. "Send a copy of your dry cleaning bill to this address." He held out the card, but she made no move to accept it.

"Thank you, but that's not necessary."

Trent let his hand fall back to his side. "At least let me replace your coffee."

The woman shook her cup. "There is a little left. I'll make my usual afternoon stop later and get more." A hint of impatience sneaked into her voice.

Turned down twice in less than three minutes; he didn't think that had ever happened to him before. He assumed either the woman didn't recognize him or was one of the few people out there who turned down a freebie when offered. Trent dropped his business card on her stacked papers. "Just in case you change your mind about the dry cleaning."

This time the woman picked up the card. "Don't worry about it. Accidents happen." She gave him a kind smile and began to turn. "Have a good afternoon."

Trent stood and watched the woman walk away, enjoying the sight of her bare legs as she headed down the sidewalk. For him, there was just something about a great pair of legs that drove him up the wall. In his hand, his phone beeped letting him know he'd received another message. After typing in a short reply, he stuck the phone in his jacket pocket and headed into the bakery.

Both his father, Supreme Court Chief Justice Mark Sherbrooke, and Marty Phillips were already seated at the glass conference table in his father's office when Trent walked in ten minutes later with a box of cannoli in one hand. He hadn't been inside the office in over a year, but by the looks of it, his stepmother, Abigail, had redecorated. All the dark wood furniture had been replaced by sleek chrome and glass. Where the leather sofa and barrel chairs had been now stood some futuristic pieces that he feared would break if an average adult male sat in them. The only thing that remained was the antique grandfather clock that Trent's mom had given his father on their last wedding anniversary before her death. The piece stood out among the ultra modern decor, but it remained a constant reminder of Donna Sherbrooke, the woman Mark Sherbrooke never stopped loving.

"Good, you're here," Mark Sherbrooke said in way of a greeting. "Have a seat."

Trent pulled out a chair at the conference table and eyed it for a moment before sitting. Then he placed the bakery box on the table.

"I arranged for lunch at noon. Your cousin Sara should be here by then." His father didn't waste any time grabbing a cannoli from the box.

Trent hadn't seen Sara in almost a year. Last he'd heard, she had moved to California to work for the governor. "She's in Rhode Island?" Although not as close to Sara as he was to her older brother Jake, he knew how knowledgeable she was when it came to Washington and politics.

Mark nodded. "She's here for a fundraiser this weekend. She offered to help when I mentioned your plans."

"We can catch her up when she arrives," Marty Phillips said, his Texas drawl coming through loud and clear.

Marty Phillips had served as his Uncle Warren's campaign advisor during his run for the Presidency. Although he'd only met him one time before, Trent hadn't questioned his father's suggestion that he hire him for his own campaign. The man had a fabulous reputation. Of the last four campaigns he'd worked on, all had been victorious, including two presidents, one senator and a governor.

With the pleasantries aside, they got down to business, beginning with who they suspected would be Trent's biggest rivals for Senator Harrison's seat. Then they proceeded to list each of their weaknesses and how they could best capitalize on them. This discussion continued until Sara arrived. Dressed in a navy blue skirt with a matching blazer, she looked every inch the sleek professional he remembered from when she worked on Senator Healy's campaign, with one exception—she looked happier than he ever saw her before.

"It's so good to see you." Sara didn't hesitate to hug him when he stood.

"You, too. I appreciate your help." On autopilot, he pulled out a chair for his cousin. Proper manners and etiquette had been drilled into all the Sherbrooke children at a young age.

"What did I miss?" Sara pulled out her computer tablet and prepared to work.

In no time, Marty recapped what they'd covered so far. "One of my biggest concerns is Trent's reputation," Marty said, turning the conversation toward a new topic. "People in this state are sick and tired of the privileged, womanizing politicians doing whatever they please. Last year's scandal involving the mayor and that model is still fresh in everyone's mind, as is the case involving Congressman Kohl and the undercover cop in January."

Trent saw one major difference between both of those men and him: they were married; he wasn't, at least not yet. Someday he'd marry. After all, there were not many successful, single politicians out there, but it wouldn't be a love match. Not that he doubted love existed. His father had certainly loved his mother, not to mention there were plenty of other examples of it in his own family. Rather, he didn't see it ever happening to him. In fact, he wasn't even sure he wanted it happening to him anyway.

His father had been crushed when his first wife died. And although he seemed happy and content with Abigail, his third wife, his second marriage to Jane had been hell from start to finish.

"If you had a stellar political background, the public might be willing to ignore the tabloid headlines, but with the exception of your family name, you're a political unknown." Marty remained expressionless as he presented his argument. "In order to win this election you'll need to win over the female voters. You'll never do that by showing up on the cover of magazines with half-naked models on your arm."

Marty's last comment stung. He couldn't control what his dates wore, and he'd hardly call any of them half-naked.

"What are your thoughts, Sara?" his father asked.

"I agree with Marty. People are tired of political scandal. They want politicians they're not embarrassed to say they voted for. Reforming Trent's reputation as a playboy would go a long way. Like Marty said, if Trent had a strong history in politics we could push that into the forefront, use it to overshadow the negative buzz from his competition, but it's just not there."

At least she didn't mention half-naked women.

"We want people to relate to Trent," Sara continued. "Coming across more like the 'boy next door' rather than the 'sleazy playboy' is one way to do that."

Wow, in less than fifteen minutes he'd been insulted by both his campaign advisor and his cousin. "What do you suggest?" he asked. If it meant winning, he'd take the experts' advice.

"First, ditch those lingerie models and empty-headed socialites you escort around," Marty answered with no hesitation.

"You want me to become a monk then? Is that what you are saying?" He'd realized even before now that he'd have to make some sacrifices in order to win, but living life in solitude didn't suit him.

Marty tapped his pen against the table. "No. Besides, everyone here knows that you'd never pull that off, and even if you did, the media wouldn't buy it." Marty twirled his pen between his fingers. "You need a way to relate to people. Make them fall in love with you. Respect you the way they respect your uncle. I suggest you find yourself a woman from a respected family and marry her. Someone well educated with connections, not one of those empty-headed models you love to date. If you marry someone the people respect, they'll respect you, too."

Sara glanced at him and then across at Marty. "You think marriage will turn around his reputation the way it did Jake's?" Sara asked in an accusing tone.

Marty gave them a curt nod. "More or less."

Sara sighed loud enough for him to hear. "I hate to admit it, but Marty's right. If you marry someone respectable it would help win over the public." She played with the giant diamond engagement ring on her left hand as she spoke.

"And as long as the woman in question understands its an arrangement going in, I see no reason you need to make a love match," Marty said. "In fact, I know several prominent families that would be interested in such an arrangement with the Sherbrooke family. And as long as you're discreet about your involvement with other women later on, they'd be willing to look the other way."

Sara shook her head. "I disagree. It has to be a real relationship and marriage. It's too late for a marriage of convenience. Trent should've done that a year or two ago. If he marries someone like Vanessa Mitchell, the voters will see through the ruse," she said referring to a prominent socialite they all knew.

"You give the voters too much credit, Sara. All they will see is a beautiful married couple."

"And you underestimate them." Sara's tone turned cold. "Sure, he'd fool some voters, but not all. He needs a real marriage, even if it means he pushes back his timetable for entering politics."

Wonderful. The two people in the room with the most political experience had polar opposite opinions. "What are your thoughts, Dad?" Thus far, his father had remained unusually quiet on the matter.

"I've always been straightforward with you regarding your relationships, and I agree your reputation might hurt your chances. If you had someone in your life like Charlie, I believe it would help win over voters. As for the rest, that's up to you. Whichever path you take, be prepared for the unexpected."

He respected his father and he valued his opinions, especially on the matter of politics. Mark Sherbrooke had spent his life around powerful politicians. That was the main reason he'd held this meeting here today rather than in his own office. If he believed Marty was correct, he'd take it into consideration.

A knock at the office door prevented Trent from responding. As lunch was set out on the conference table, his mind weighed the pros and cons of what had been discussed so far. Finding and falling in love with someone was unlikely, even if he wanted to follow Sara's suggestions. After not finding love for so long, he figured he didn't even know how to go about it, which left Marty's plan. Assuming he stayed honest and up front with the woman, he had no problem carrying out a charade. They could set it up like a business contract. "Who do you have in mind, Marty?"

———

ADDISON TOSSED the ruined paperwork onto her desk. Once she reprinted the pages she'd have to transfer her notes onto the fresh copies. Thankfully, she could still read them. While the printer worked at spitting out clean copies, she grabbed the white blouse she kept in her office closet. She'd learned at her first professional job the importance of keeping a clean set of clothes in the office. It'd been only her second day at Ducat and Wakefield Designers. She'd been eating her lunch at Quincy Market when a young child had tripped and spilled an entire container of chocolate milk on her lap. She'd had to buy an entire new outfit before returning to work that day. Ever since then, she'd kept an extra outfit at work.

After slipping on the clean top, she stuffed the coffee-stained shirt in a bag with a tiny shake of her head. *Dry-cleaned. Yeah, right.* She didn't own anything that required dry cleaning. Heck, that particular top didn't even require an iron, making it one of her favorites. In fact, she owned three just like it only in different colors because she could literally pull it from the clothes dryer and slip it on. Someone like Trent Sherbrooke most likely had all his clothing dry-cleaned or at least washed and ironed for him. The brief thought of the man caused an image to form in her head. Over the years she'd seen plenty of photographs of the handsome billionaire. Most of the time some equally beautiful woman hung off his arm. The pictures hadn't done him justice. She'd never seen anyone with eyes that shade of blue, and his face, well, she didn't even know where to begin. Looking at him had been like looking at perfection. As if some great master sculptor had carved him, making sure each feature complimented the others. Her fingers itched at the thought of sketching a picture of him.

Addie dropped into her seat and reached for what was left of her coffee. *Time to get back to work.* She needed to finish this proposal before her meeting with the homeowners tomorrow. Although the project wouldn't be as large as some of the ones she'd worked on while at Ducat and Wakefield, it'd bring in money and keep her business going. Everyone had to start somewhere. With any luck, in another year or so she'd have enough of a reputation to attract big projects like those she'd worked on in Boston, and then she could hire more employees. Right now the whole company consisted of herself and her part-time assistant, Tara. Of course, if she moved her office out of the city to an area with lower rent it would help, but she couldn't bring herself to do it. She loved working in the city. It stimulated her, got her creative side flowing. On more than one occasion she'd be at home struggling on a project and the minute she walked into her office the ideas started to flow. Moving her office out of downtown Providence was an absolute last resort.

She read over the notes she already jotted down, then pulled up the digital photos she'd taken at the Lancaster's home.

"The curtains you ordered for the Wagners won't be ready until next week," Tara said, stepping into her office. A college student at Rhode Island School of Design, Tara worked at the office four days a week. "But the painters can start on Friday if that works for the Vonns."

Addie ran the information through her head. The late delivery would set the project back a bit, but she didn't think the Wagners would mind much. So far the couple had been remarkably easy to work with. "Okay. Can you call the Vonns and see if the painter can start then, and I'll contact the Wagners." Right now she had two ongoing projects and if the Lancasters liked her proposal tomorrow that would make three solid deals.

"Will do. Is there anything you need before I leave?"

Addie thought about the other office-related tasks that needed to be done that week, but she remained silent. If she asked Tara to stay and help, she would, but Addie couldn't afford the extra pay. And even though Tara would say it wasn't necessary, Addie wouldn't feel right not paying the younger woman.

"No. I'm all set with everything else. Thanks."

Once Tara returned to her own desk, Addie called the Wagners to break the bad news. As she expected they were fine with the minor delay, which was a relief. Over the years she'd seen some clients become irate when projects didn't go as planned. Sometimes they demanded discounts because of delays. She'd even seen some break contracts. While Ducat and Wakefield could survive with such financial losses, she couldn't, at least not at this point.

With the phone call out of the way, she lost herself in the proposal for the Lancaster home. Before she left today, she wanted it done.

———

"HOW LONG ARE YOU AROUND FOR?" Trent and Sara had left his father's office and returned to his downtown apartment.

"About a week. The governor is on vacation with his family in Hawaii. Christopher is arriving tomorrow and since everyone is at Cliff House, we thought we'd visit for a few days then head over to Martha's Vineyard. Jake and Charlie plan to stay until Sunday, and then they are heading to North Salem to see her family. I don't know how long Dylan and Callie plan to stay."

Trent made a mental note of everyone's plans. At some point between today and the weekend, he'd make an effort to get to Newport. "I appreciate your input today," he said. "If you weren't working for the governor, I'd ask you to run my campaign."

Sara played with the engagement ring on her finger, a thoughtful expression on her face. "So you're definitely going to run?"

Trent leaned forward and rested his forearms on the table. "You don't think it's a good idea?"

Across from him, she shook her head. "If it's what you want, I say go for it. Just think hard before you sign on with Marty."

The only time he heard anything negative about Marty Phillips it came from the candidates that ran against whoever hired him. "He was your father's campaign advisor, and he's got a great reputation. I don't see a problem."

"He knows what he is doing and he gets results," Sara said. "Sometimes his methods are questionable. If you want more details, ask Dylan."

Now she really had him curious. "Come on, Sara. Out with it." He doubted he'd get anything else from Sara. She'd always been good at keeping a secret, even as a child.

Sara took a sip from her tea before she answered. "You'll have to ask Dylan, Trent. But take Marty's insistence today that you get married."

"You didn't think the idea of marriage was terrible."

"And I still don't, but a real marriage not some sham. You can't use someone like that."

"Sara, you wouldn't have said that a year ago."

"I might have been more open to the idea," Sara replied. "But even then I would have thought there wasn't enough time to pull it off."

If he took Marty's advice, he didn't plan to use anyone. He'd be upfront about the whole thing from the beginning. People might call him a lot of things, but he wasn't cruel. "If they know going in, Sara, no one will get hurt. I haven't decided yet, but if I take Marty's advice, it'll be like a business deal."

Sara actually rolled her eyes at him, reminding him of his younger sister, Allison. "Falling in love and getting married wouldn't kill you. Jake was almost as bad as you when it came to women and look how happy he is now."

The number of women that had passed through his cousin's life didn't even come close to his. Although Jake had been known as a playboy, much of his reputation had been exaggerated. The same couldn't be said for him.

"I don't think I'm cut out for a relationship like Jake's. I have never met a woman I could picture spending the rest of my life with," he said. "And since we're talking about marriage, have you and Christopher set a date yet?" Anything was better than having yet another female relative lecture him about how he lived his life. "Or are you taking a page out of Jake's book?"

"Do you even need to ask? I don't think my mom has completely forgiven Jake yet," Sara answered. "We picked June 23 for the wedding. Mom says it isn't enough time, but I'm not worried."

TWO

EVERYTHING in the office had a feminine touch to it, yet it remained just neutral enough that if anyone walked in they wouldn't think he'd taken over someone's office. Of course that was exactly what he'd done. Now that he'd turned his position over to his brother Gray, he needed to ground himself here in Rhode Island if he hoped to make his way into the Senate.

This new position as Regional Director for the Northeast at Sherbrooke Enterprises would allow him to solidify his presences in the state. At the same time, the position gave him a new challenge and allowed him to be closer to family. As much as he'd loved his previous job, it no longer possessed any challenges and it kept him away from his loved ones. Now he worked just blocks from his father and floors above his Aunt Marilyn, who was the director of The Helping Hands Foundation. Originally started during the Great Depression by his great-grandmother to help provide for homeless families, the organization had grown over the years. When his grandmother stepped down as director in the eighties, his own mother had taken her place and expanded the foundation even more. Following her death, his father's sister, Marilyn, had taken over as director, and today the foundation provided help to homeless shelters, public schools, youth programs, and senior centers.

Yes, the change was for the better, but something had to be done about this office. Next week he'd have his secretary contact some local interior designers. Trent dismissed all thoughts of his office and grabbed the top folder in his inbox. Several area hotels were set for renovations in the upcoming months and he wanted to review the final proposals before he signed off on anything. After that, he would start on the proposal for the new luxury resort proposed for Ogunquit, Maine.

As he turned to the second page for a Sherbrooke Express Hotel located in Hartford, there was a knock on the door. "Come in," he said as he continued to read.

"Mr. Jackman from Guardian Construction called. He rescheduled your meeting until next week. I already updated your calendar," Shirley said. "And Mrs. Belmont's office called. She wanted to know if you'd be available for lunch this afternoon."

Trent eyed the stack of folders before him. "Not today. See if tomorrow works." He enjoyed spending time with his Aunt Marilyn but needed to get caught up. According to the date stamp on some of the proposals, they'd come in several months ago, well before the previous regional director left. "What exactly did Monica do anyway? Some of the proposals I read through last night came in five months ago."

Shirley, who had worked as assistant to Monica as well as the director before that, glanced at the folders. "She was out a lot after she became pregnant. In the past I helped Monica with these, so if you want I can take some of the proposals and go through them."

As tempting an offer as it was, Trent shook his head. "You have your own responsibilities. I'll handle this."

A look of relief passed across the forty-something-year-old assistant's face. "Please let me know if you change your mind."

Once Shirley left, Trent returned his attention to the Hartford project. Once he completed that one, he grabbed the next project in the stack. Like the ones he'd looked through the night before, most of the renovations were standard updates. Still, he didn't want to make any assumptions about the ones he'd yet to read. So one by one, he made his way through the stack, working through lunch and into the early evening. By doing so, he managed to complete a nice chunk of work.

Trent rubbed his eyes. He'd read so much today his eyes burned. Tomorrow he'd tackle the rest. Right now he needed some food and maybe a coffee or two. Otherwise, he risked falling asleep on the way to his stepmother's get together later tonight.

"I'll see you in the morning." Trent stopped at Shirley's desk located just outside his door. Despite it being well past five o'clock, the woman remained. His first day at the office when he'd left at six and she'd still been working, he'd questioned it. Evidently, Shirley had school-age children and acted as her daughter's soccer coach and her son's Cub Scout leader. In order to make it to those things, she left early on Mondays and Wednesdays, but stayed late on Tuesdays and Thursdays to make up the hours. Since the schedule had been in place for a few years and seemed to work, he saw no reason to change it.

Shirley glanced over at him and smiled. "Have a nice evening, Mr. Sherbrooke."

The heat and humidity broke over him like a wave when he stepped outside. Inside his cool air-conditioned office, he'd forgotten about the heat wave that gripped much of Southern New England. Thankfully, Ambrosia Pastry Shop and Cafe was only a few streets over.

By the time he reached the bakery door, sweat dripped down his back making his undershirt stick to his skin. The smells drifting out of the bakery made the unpleasant situation well worth it. Just as he was about to enter, a woman with two children in a stroller appeared. Stepping to the side, he held open the door for her and then followed inside. As he waited for his turn, his eyes swept over the store. Several college-aged customers sat at the various tables. Some shared the extra large desserts while others studied and drank coffee as they ate freshly made panini.

"Did Uncle put something different in these?"

The female voice grabbed his attention and had him looking back at the table closest to him. The woman who sat there had her back toward him so he couldn't see her face, but the voice and hair he recognized. Or at least he thought he did. Was that the same woman he'd bumped into earlier that week? She'd mentioned she worked in the area, and while he'd kept an eye out for her over the past week, he'd never seen her again.

"He added some coconut water to the batter. How is it?" a woman dressed in an Ambrosia T-shirt answered from the next table as she washed it down.

"They're amazing."

It had to be the same person. Stepping out of line, he walked around to the table prepared to say hello, until he remembered he didn't know her name. Not that something like that ever stopped him from talking to a woman. "You're a regular here, too?"

The woman's head snapped up. "You could say that. Besides, no one makes better Italian wedding cookies than this bakery."

"Do you mind if I sit? I promise not to spill anything on you this time." He let his mouth curve into a smile.

The woman moved the unopened magazines on the table. "Have a seat. I already finished my coffee so it's probably safe," she said with a straight face despite the laughter dancing in her eyes.

"That puts my mind at ease." Trent sat down before he continued. "I don't think I got your name the other day."

"My name is Addison, but my friends usually call me Addie." Addie closed the magazine she had open and added it to her pile.

He'd given her his business card the other day but it seemed appropriate to give her his name now anyway. "It's nice to see you again. I'm Trent." He stuck out his hand.

Addie accepted and out of habit his eyes went to her left hand, which was bare of any rings. "You didn't get burned the other day, did you?" The day following the incident he'd expected a phone call from a law office saying he was being sued for scalding a woman with hot coffee.

Addie shook her head, a stray piece of chestnut-colored hair falling over her forehead. "Believe it or not, I've spilled hotter coffee on myself before." She tucked the hair back behind her ear.

"I'm serious about the top. Please send the bill to me." His stomach growled when a student walked by carrying a slice of Tiramisu.

"The stains came out in the wash. I wore the top again yesterday."

His mouth watered when he caught a glimpse of a pizza going by. "I need something to eat. Can I get you anything? Another coffee?" If he couldn't cover the dry cleaning bill at least he could buy her a coffee today.

For a few seconds she considered his words. "If you think that's safe," she said with humor in her voice. "Otherwise, some water would be great, too."

"Since we're both seated I think we're okay. How do you like your coffee?"

"Extra light with sugar."

"Be right back." Trent stood and rejoined the line at the counter.

A few minutes later, he placed a plastic tray with two mugs of coffee and a spinach pie on the table. "Maybe you should take your coffee off yourself."

With a small chuckle she reached for the extra light coffee. "Excellent choice. I had that for lunch yesterday."

"You do come in here a lot." Trent wasted no time taking a bite of his food.

"My office isn't far from here so I'm here at least once a day." She popped another piece of her cookie in her mouth and then washed it down with her coffee. "The girl that just finished washing the tables is my cousin and the woman that waited on you is my aunt. My uncle is probably back in the kitchen." Addie took another sip from her coffee. "I don't remember ever seeing you in here before. And trust me, I'd remember."

"Whenever I visit my father's office I stop in. Now that I'm working in the city, I'll be around more." Trent tore his spinach pie in half.

"Thanks for the warning. I'll make sure to pay extra attention when I'm walking around here from now on," Addie said, her voice lighthearted.

Trent smiled and took a good look at the woman seated across from him. Thanks to his behavior over the years and his well-earned reputation, most women, especially unmarried ones, flirted with him or made outright sexual overtures. Except for perhaps his younger sister Allison, no females ever razzed him with slightly insulting jokes. And he liked it. In fact, he liked that he could just sit and enjoy coffee with a woman who didn't seem to expect anything but perhaps a conversation from him.

"You mentioned your office isn't far from here. Who do you work for?"

Addie wiped her hands on her napkin. "Myself now. I used to work for Ducat and Wakefield Designers in Boston, but I opened my own office here two years ago."

"You must be talented. My stepmother hired them to redecorate their estate on the Cape. She insisted they were the best."

A hint of pink colored Addie's cheeks and she glanced down. "I worked on that project. It was one of the last ones I worked on before I left. It's a gorgeous estate."

The color on her face intrigued him. He'd never seen anyone

blush from a mere compliment. "Why did you leave?" He reached for the other half of his food, content to sit and continue their conversation.

Across from him, Addie folded and unfolded the cover of a magazine. "I wanted more control. I learned a lot working for Ducat and Wakefield, but they keep all their employees on a tight leash. All ideas need to be approved by management before they can be presented to clients. Working for myself, I can work closely with my clients. Really get to know them. It makes it easier." Addie glanced down at her wristwatch and pushed back her chair.

"I need to go. I have an appointment to get to, but thank you for the coffee." She stood and grabbed her magazines.

On instinct, Trent came to his feet. "Anytime."

With a smile, she pushed in her chair and began to turn away.

Once again it struck him how different she was. She hadn't slipped him her phone number or intentionally prolonged their time together. "My new office needs a make over. Would you be interested?" His office did need a facelift, and he didn't want this to be their last conversation. He'd enjoyed it too much for that.

Addie's eyes widen just enough to reveal her true feelings.

"Yes," she answered without any hesitation.

"Great. I'll have my assistant call your office and schedule an appointment. Do you have a business card?"

After a few seconds of digging around in her purse, she held out a card.

"Excellent. Shirley will be in touch with you on Monday."

"Sounds good. Have a nice weekend."

Once she disappeared out the door, he took his seat again. Reaching for his coffee, he looked at the ivory business card in his hand. The words Designs by Addison in bold black script took up much of the space and in the bottom right hand corner her contact information and address were printed.

ADDIE HADN'T EVEN MADE it out of the parking lot behind her office building when her phone rang. She pulled out the phone as she turned onto Atwells Avenue. "Hi, Chloe," she said, recognizing the number on the screen.

"How in the world did you end up having coffee with Trent Sherbrooke?" her cousin asked, not bothering with a polite hello first.

The car in front of her moved when the light changed, and she took her foot off the break. "We sort of bumped into each other earlier this week and he spilled my coffee." Just as she approached the intersection, the light turned red again. "Darn it." Friday traffic sucked. She should have been paying closer attention to the time. If she were lucky, she'd make it to the other Ambrosia bakery located in Providence just in time for her shift. Her mother managed the first store opened by her great-grandfather in the Federal Hill section of the city and she noticed if an employee was even a few minutes late.

"I guess that explains how you met but not why he sat and had coffee with you."

The light changed again and Addie crossed the intersection. In the distance she could see the archway and the giant bronze pine nut that welcomed everyone to the Federal Hill section of Providence. "He wanted to make sure I hadn't gotten burned and he offered to have my blouse cleaned."

A sigh came through the phone. "I wish someone like that would check on me. So what's he like?"

"Nice." Addie turned into the tiny lot behind the building. According to the dashboard clock, she'd have just enough time to change her clothes before her shift started.

"That's all you have to say? This is Trent Sherbrooke we are talking about. He dated that princess from Denmark last year.

You know, the one that no one can figure out how to pronounce her name."

"I don't have time now, Chloe," Addie said as she pulled open the back door into the kitchen. "I'll call you this weekend."

"You better."

In less time than it took Clark Kent to change into Superman, Addie changed out of her skirt and top and into jean shorts and a black Ambrosia T-shirt. She'd told Trent she had an appointment. While it hadn't been a lie, it hadn't been the complete truth either. Several times a week she worked at the bakery as a way to supplement her income. So much of what her business brought in went right back into the company that she had little left over for her own personal expenses. When she'd worked in Boston money hadn't been an issue. They'd paid her well enough right out of college that she'd quit working at the bakery. Someday she hoped that would be the case again. Until then, her job in the family business allowed her to squeak by month to month.

"Great, you're here," Marta Raimono, Addie's mom, said when she spotted her in the kitchen. "I need you to start on the cannoli for the Eckhart bridal shower tomorrow."

Thank you. If she had to work at the bakery, she preferred to stay in the back out of sight. On the rare occasions she worked out front, she worried someone she'd either worked with in Boston or someone she'd done design work for would show up and recognize her. Granted, in the two years she'd been back it had only happened once, but that was once too often for her. Even now, when she thought about the afternoon Sue Adamson walked in, she cringed. Both of them had been hired by Ducat and Wakefield Designers right after graduation. In the beginning they'd been friends, bouncing ideas off each other and getting to know the city together. Despite Addie being the more talented of the two, Sue began to get more and more high profile accounts. At first she hadn't been able to figure out why. When Raphael Ducat, one of the partners, filed for divorce and then suddenly started showing up everywhere with Sue glued to his side, Addie, along with everyone else, figured out the secret to Sue's sudden success.

Addie slipped an apron over her head as she headed for the long prep table in the back. Already her mom had pulled out trays of unfilled cannoli shells. As she settled into a routine, her thoughts turned away from Sue and toward the gentleman she'd had coffee with that afternoon. In all honesty, she'd never expected to see Trent again. When she looked up and saw him standing there she'd almost fallen from her seat. At first she feared he was a figment of her imagination. After all, since their run in, she had thought of him often. She'd even caved in and sketched him two nights earlier. When he'd asked to sit down, it had taken several seconds for her brain to get a response out of her mouth. As they sat and talked she forced herself to not stare at him, which had been no easy task. He, like everyone else in his family, looked as if they belonged in the movies. For as long as she could remember, pictures of him and others in the Sherbrooke family had been in the media and, unless they had some secret family member locked up somewhere, the entire family was stunning.

Then, as if that hadn't been enough, he'd asked if she'd be interested in a job. Her first instinct had been to throw her arms around him and shout "yes." Talk about excellent publicity for her business. Somehow though, she'd controlled herself and offered up a simple yes. But even now as she considered the possibility of working for Trent Sherbrooke, her excitement grew. If she redecorated his office and he liked it, she could have other high profile clients knocking on her office door.

"Wow, you're halfway done already."

Her mom's voice caused her hands to still and she glanced down at the shells on the table. Sure enough, one whole tray was finished. "I guess I got into a good rhythm."

Her mom patted her arm. "When you're done with that can you start on the biscotti. I need two dozen hazelnut and two dozen almond for tomorrow."

With a nod, Addie slipped back into autopilot. She'd been filling cannoli shells since she was twelve years old and could do it half-asleep at this point. As she reached for another shell, her mind went back to how her business might benefit if she completed a project for Trent Sherbrooke.

THREE

TRENT PASSED through the secret service agents posted at the gates of Cliff House and followed the winding driveway toward the garage. As the mansion came into view, he slowed. It'd been at least a year since he'd last visited, and he'd forgotten just how grand the old mansion was. In fact, it'd give the grand estates he'd visited while in England and France a run for their money.

Accelerating once more, he took the final bend in the driveway, pulled in alongside a black Aston Martin, and then he killed the engine. Once outside he took his time as he walked toward the main house. Unlike in the city, a cool breeze came up off the ocean, making the hot July day bearable despite the high humidity.

Like magic, the massive front door opened before he even reached for the handle and his uncle's solemn-faced butler greeted him. "Good afternoon, Mr. Sherbrooke. Your aunt has been expecting you." The man spoke in his ever-constant monotone voice as he stepped inside. "Everyone is out on the veranda," the man said as he closed the door.

Trent passed through the familiar halls. As a child he and his siblings spent countless days at the mansion visiting with their cousins. Only when he'd hit his teens had his visits become less frequent, as he chose to spend his vacations from school in more exotic locations.

"Look who decided to grace us with his presence," Jake said good-naturedly when Trent stepped outside.

After giving Jake a friendly thump on the back, Trent took a seat at the table. "I knew how devastated you'd all be if you didn't see me before you left." Of all his cousins, he was closest to Jake. Less than a year older than Jake, he'd spent much of his childhood with him. Later they'd attended the same boarding school in Connecticut. During college they'd seen less of each other. While Trent had attended Harvard like so many other Sherbrookes, his cousin had gone to Caltech. After graduation, they once again spent much of their time together visiting the same nightclubs and casinos. These days, though, they rarely saw each other. In fact, the last time he'd seen Jake had been more than a year and half ago at a New Year's Eve party.

"It is wonderful to see you. I feared you wouldn't make it before I leave," Elizabeth Sherbrooke said, her voice still accented although she'd lived in the United States for over thirty years. "Your uncle is expecting me back in Washington tomorrow."

He'd hoped to see his uncle that weekend. Ever since his conversation with Sara regarding Marty Phillips he'd wanted to get his uncle's opinion. His absence today came as no shock, however. No matter how important the cause, his uncle couldn't attend every fundraiser the family sponsored now that he was president.

"Have you met everyone?" Elizabeth asked.

"Everyone except Prince Charming's wife," he said, using the nickname the media had given his cousin years earlier.

Jake gave him a dirty look, then turned to the redhead seated next to him. "Charlie, this is my cousin Trent."

The woman extended her hand toward him. "It's nice to meet

you. Jake's told me a lot about you." She gave him a smile that indicated her husband had shared a lot of personal information with her, including some he'd probably wished Jake hadn't.

Trent accepted the woman's hand. "It's great to finally meet you. We'll have to talk later. I have some stories that I could share with you that I bet Jake has never mentioned."

"Hey, Trent. Sara said you might stop by." Christopher Hall appeared at the doorway. "Nice to see you again," he said as he joined everyone at the table.

He'd known Jake's former college roommate and best friend for several years. In fact, on numerous occasions they'd prowled the Los Angles nightclubs together. "Congratulations on the engagement." When the three of them had hung out together, Christopher had always been the one he imagined settled and married someday. He'd just never imagined it would be to his younger cousin Sara. Yet the two appeared happy and in love.

"Sara said you decided to run for Senate."

Trent looked over at Dylan, his uncle's stepson and his cousin's husband. He'd known Dylan all his life and considered him family. Other than himself, he'd thought Dylan the least likely of everyone gathered at the table to ever marry. Now the no-nonsense executive sat with an arm around his pregnant wife's shoulders. Talk about times changing.

With a nod, he answered. "Yes, I've hired Marty Phillips to run my campaign. My father and I met with him earlier this week."

Across the table Callie frowned and glanced over at Sara, but remained silent.

"Good luck. If there's anything I can do, let me know," Dylan said, his subtle English accent lacing his voice.

"Same here, Trent." Jake's voice pulled his attention away from Dylan and Callie.

During the two years he'd worked on overseas projects for Sherbrooke Enterprises, he'd made few trips back to visit family.

Now once again surrounded by his cousins, he realized how much he'd missed his family.

"Warren is pleased with your decision," his aunt said. "He spoke with your father earlier this week."

His Aunt Elizabeth's comment came as no surprise. The Sherbrooke family had been involved in politics for years. In a way it was expected that at least one Sherbrooke male from each generation would get involved in politics. For the longest time his aunt and uncle had hoped Jake would follow in the family tradition even though he'd never displayed an interest. For Trent it'd always been in the back of his mind, but until that past spring he hadn't been ready to take the plunge. Instead, he'd been content with his position at Sherbrooke Enterprises and his rather carefree lifestyle. When Callie and Dylan announced her pregnancy though, a switch had gone on inside him. He'd taken a good look around and realized that everyone he cared about was making these grand changes in their lives except him.

"Thanks, Trent. Now they'll stop harassing me about it," Jake said.

"You're father hasn't mentioned it to you in a long time Jake." Trent's aunt said from the head of the table. "He's accepted that you have no interest in politics."

Jake looked over at him. "A long time to them means six months. But now, thanks to you, the heats off me. I owe you one."

"Don't worry. I'll hold you to that."

ADDIE RECORDED the last two deposits she'd made into her company checking account. Once she verified that the balance on her spreadsheet matched the one on the bank's website, she turned her attention to her monthly bills. Both her rent and electric bill were due, as were a handful of bills to contractors.

Whenever this time of the month rolled around she cursed herself for going out on her own. Handling the money side of the business was her least favorite part of her job. She found it not only depressing to see the balance in her account go down, but also tedious. Several months before she started her own company she'd taken a few accounting classes at the local community college. It'd had taken all of her self-discipline to complete them. How anyone majored in accounting and then spent the rest of their working life elbow-deep in numbers was beyond her. If at some point she made enough, she planned to hire someone to take care of all the financial aspects of her company.

Do a good job for Trent Sherbrooke and perhaps that accountant will be in the future even sooner. Addie stuffed the check she'd written into the envelope, her mind going back to Trent. What kind of office would he prefer? Did he like a more traditional style or would his tastes lean toward the ultra-contemporary? Not that it mattered. She'd learned long ago to put aside her own personal tastes and focus on the client. It had been something she'd struggled with on her first few jobs after college. Now though, her personal views stayed safely under lock and key. Even still, she found the projects she enjoyed the most were ones that were more in line with her own preferences.

Right before she left Ducat and Wakefield, she worked with a couple that had purchased a lovely home in Wellesley, which in her opinion hadn't needed anything. Without even moving into the home, the couple called the firm requesting a complete redesign. They'd wanted the entire first floor opened up and then redecorated. By the end of the project, they'd knocked down walls and added windows making the first floor look like one giant room. Then they added futuristic-looking furniture and lots of stainless steel. By the time Addie finished work on the home, it reminded her of some exhibit from a "houses of the future" display. The couple had loved it and had even given her a rave review, which had pleased her supervisors.

She hoped Trent preferred a more traditional decorating style. It would make the process all the more enjoyable. Maybe almost as enjoyable as looking at him. As much as she didn't judge a person on looks alone, she'd loved looking at him that day over coffee. She'd found it difficult to look away from his dark blue, almost sapphire-colored eyes. The sun had bronzed his face, its features rugged and sensual at the same time. His strong jaw and chin hinted at a stubborn streak and his mouth, oh man, she could have watched his lips move all day.

Addie slipped her checkbook back into her desk and let herself daydream for a little longer. Yes, he was by far the most gorgeous man she'd ever spoken with. Why couldn't some of the men she came in contact with on a daily basis look like that? Then again, perhaps it was better that they didn't. Otherwise she, along with the rest of the female population, would never get any work done.

"Addie," Tara said from the other side of the door, interrupting her daydream.

"Come on in." She'd have to fantasize again later.

"Here's today's mail." Tara placed a stack of envelopes and the day's newspaper on her desk.

"Thanks." She started sifting through the envelopes, sorting them into two piles, one for bills and another for junk mail. Even at work she received junk mail. Perhaps even more than at home.

"Could I check out the society section of the paper? My cousin's wedding announcement should be in there."

Addie reached for the paper at the bottom of her pile. She didn't even know why she bothered with it. She rarely read it anymore. "You can keep it." She tugged the society section from the paper and her mouth dropped open.

"What's wrong?"

In silence, Addie turned the page toward Tara.

"Is that you and Trent Sherbrooke?"

Addie nodded, unable to speak, then she turned the paper back around hoping the picture had changed. Unfortunately, it remained the same a photo of her and Trent enjoying coffee at Ambrosia with the headline "Coffee For Two: Legendary playboy cozies up with local small business owner."

"Wow. I can't believe you met him. What's he like?"

Why would someone take and send in the picture? How had they known her name? Both her name and company name were stated in the article under the picture.

"Addie?" Tara asked again.

"What?" She tore her eyes from the paper.

"What's he like?"

Addie rubbed her forehead as a headache started. "Nice. Or at least he seemed that way." She scanned the article, then put the paper down. "This is awful."

"It doesn't seem that bad to me." Tara picked up the discarded paper. "It's not like you're sitting with a serial killer or anything. I wouldn't worry about it."

Not worry about it? Someone not only took her picture but also passed it on. How could she not worry?

FOUR

A KNOCK on his office door drew Trent's attention away from the documents on his desk.

"Marty Phillips is here to see you," Shirley said after she opened the door.

"Send him in, Shirley." Absorbed in his work, he'd lost track of time. He'd intended to grab a quick lunch before his meeting with Marty. "And when you get a chance, order me a lunch, please. The same thing I had on Tuesday. Check with Marty and see if he wants anything."

With a nod, Shirley moved away from the door, and seconds later Marty entered. Immediately, Sara's warning surfaced. Despite his insistence, she still refused to elaborate on her comments from the other day, but even so, she'd made her feelings clear. Maybe he should have questioned Dylan at Cliff House.

"It's nice to see you again." Trent stood and ignored the questions in his gut when he considered the purpose of their meeting. Marty had compiled a list of potential marriage candidates in record time. Today they'd go through it and select one. As he came around his desk, he lowered the knot in his tie a fraction of an inch. If he wanted to win, this was what he needed to do.

He'd reminded himself of that over and over ever since Marty confirmed this meeting with him. Even Sara believed a steady relationship and then marriage was the best way to repair his image. Of course, she disagreed with this method, but she was biased. If Marty felt this was the best course of action, he'd go with it. After all, many politicians had this man to thank for their positions.

Marty dropped his briefcase on the conference table near the windows. "I put together comprehensive binders on three potential wives." He pulled out the spiral bound binders and placed them on the table as he sat. "But I have another idea that trumps the entire thing."

Intrigued, Trent took the seat across from the campaign advisor. Before today Marty had been dead set on the idea of a marriage. What could've changed his mind?

"Did you by any chance see the society section in yesterday's *Providence Gazette*?"

Trent shook his head and waited. He didn't even remember that the *Gazette* had a society section.

Across the table Marty pulled something else from his briefcase. "Forget about the women listed in those." He pointed to the binders he'd first tossed down. "This is who I want you to win over and marry." He held out a section of the newspaper and pointed to a picture that filled much of the page. "A similar picture showed up in the *Boston Times* this morning."

Trent grabbed the paper, the headline over the picture taunting him. "Coffee For Two: Legendary playboy cozies up with local small business owner."

"How the hell is this possible? There were no photographers around." At least he didn't think so, yet there was no mistaking the picture of Addison and him having coffee at Ambrosia.

"My sources at the papers refused to give me a name but told me a customer took the picture. That doesn't matter." Marty pointed at Addison in the picture. "She's perfect. I've already run a background check on her. She'll remind people of your cousin Callie and Jake's wife, Charlie. You know how much the public adores them. They didn't even care that Callie was illegitimate. All they cared about was that your uncle pulled her into the family fold. And society loves that Charlie, one of its own, tamed Prince Charming. The only time you see Jake in the news these days is when The Falmouth Foundation takes action."

He couldn't disagree with how much the American public adored the two women, but he'd just wrapped his head around Marty's initial plan.

Marty pulled two folders from his briefcase and slid one toward him. "Some of the information in here you may already know, but I'll give you the condensed version. You can read the rest later." He opened his own folder. "Born Addison Raimono to Marta and Salvatore Raimono. She has no criminal record. She earned her bachelor's degree from Suffolk University in interior design. Two years ago she started her own business, Designs by Addison. It does both interior design and decorating, although she's handled more decorating projects since the business started." Marty paused for a breath. "While the company regularly has clients, she's just getting by. Several times a week she works at one of her family's bakeries, usually the one on Federal Hill. My guess is to supplement her income. For the past two years she's lived in Cumberland." Marty turned the page in his folder and kept on reading. "Her mother runs the family bakery located up on Federal Hill and her father, a retired Marine, works as a correctional officer at the Maximum Security prison in Cranston."

Trent followed along, amazed at how much information Marty had gathered in such a short amount of time.

"Addison is the youngest of five children and her family has strong ties to Rhode Island. Her mother's grandfather, Giovanni

D'Ambrosia came to this country and opened the first Ambrosia Pastry Shop and Cafe on Federal Hill. Later, his son opened another store in the North End of Boston. The third location on Benefit Street, where this picture was taken, opened twenty-five years ago and the family has just rented a location at Quincy Market for a fourth." Marty took a sip from the coffee he'd brought in with him. "All that information is in your folder. You can read through everything again later."

Marty fell silent when someone knocked on the door. As Shirley entered and laid out lunch, Trent looked back at the newspaper, his blood pressure inching skyward. Most of the time he ignored headlines. Rather than let them bother him, he let the comments roll off his back regardless of whether or not they were true. But this headline couldn't have come at a worse time. It especially angered him because all they'd done was have a coffee and talk for a few minutes.

"You dug up all this information but couldn't learn who leaked this picture to the papers?" he asked when the door closed behind his assistant.

Marty folded up the sleeves of his shirt. "It's all a matter of importance. The who doesn't matter. The wonderful opportunity it presents does. Now, I need to know everything. How did you meet her? How long have you known her? Have you slept with her yet?"

Trent pinched the bridge of his nose. *Christ, couldn't he have a cup of coffee with a woman without someone assuming he'd slept with her?* "I met her just before you and I met last week. I bumped into her on the sidewalk and spilled coffee on her. When this picture was taken I had stopped in the bakery and when I saw her again I said hello. We talked for a few minutes before she left."

As Marty chewed he jotted notes down on a legal pad. "That's it? You didn't ask her out to dinner? Get her phone number?"

Did the man think he asked out every attractive female he met? "More or less."

Marty looked up at him. "More or less, I need to know everything. And when I say everything, I mean it."

"I told her I wanted this office redecorated and asked if she might be interested. Shirley called and set up an appointment with her." After giving Shirley the instructions, he hadn't thought anymore about it.

"Excellent. When?"

"I'll have to check my calendar."

Marty tapped his pen against his pad several times before he spoke. "We might have to change our timetable a little, but I'd like to keep to it if possible. A wedding at the end of next summer is ideal. That would give you a solid year of marriage before the actual election."

Caution flags jumped up as he listened to Marty. The advisor's original plan had been acceptable. A marriage to a wealthy socialite who viewed their relationship as a way to achieve her own goals was one thing. What Marty proposed now was entirely something else.

"Perhaps we should stick with what we originally discussed. Why don't I go through these and pick a candidate?" Trent reached for the binders Marty had put together. "Then there'll be no need to adjust our timeline."

"You hired me because you want to win." Marty pointed his pen at the picture of Addison. "She's your ticket to the Senate."

Trent's eyes focused on the picture. What had she just said to him when the picture was taken? It must have been funny because he had a huge smile on his face. Come to think of it, he'd smiled through much of their conversation. She'd had an easygoing nature with a great sense of humor. There had been no awkward moments or long gaps of silence. Under different circumstances he wouldn't mind getting to know her better.

"The women in here may help repair your reputation." Marty

pointed to the binders he'd put together of potential wife candidates. "This one, though, will win the hearts of voters." He nodded toward the newspaper on the table. "I don't understand the problem. She's beautiful and well-educated."

Marty had him there. Addison was attractive and, from all he could tell, intelligent. Even with that knowledge, a corner of his conscience prickled at the idea.

Across the table Marty popped a pickle in his mouth and chewed as he waited. "If it helps, look at it this way. Her involvement with you will put her business on the fast track. The whole thing will still more or less be a business agreement."

Trent nodded. Marty had a point. If he and Addison became romantically involved it would do more for her business than an ad during the Super Bowl.

"If you're going to make it in politics you need to learn to do what's right for your career, everything else comes second. Trust me, I've been around long enough to know that few politicians make it with their conscience intact." Marty pushed the paper closer to him. "So what's it going to be?"

Addison's face beamed up at him. "We'll try it your way, but if it's not working we will fall back to our original plan." Sure, they'd had an enjoyable conversation over coffee, but he was not prepared to wager the rest of his life on that. He picked up his untouched sandwich. "I'm assuming you made sure she's not involved with anyone."

The look Marty gave him said it all. "Unless she's got a secret lover tucked in her closet, she's single and has been for over a year."

"Okay, I'll let you know how things go. But in the meantime, keep working on who leaked this picture."

THE PHONE on Addie's desk rang again. In fact, her office phone hadn't stopped ringing since yesterday. It seemed like suddenly everyone in the greater Providence area wanted their home or office redecorated. While she knew her reputation was growing, she knew that wasn't the reason for her sudden popularity. When she'd first seen her picture in the paper she wanted to crawl under a rock. The idea that someone took her picture without her knowledge and then sold it outraged her, made her feel violated. Yet since that picture surfaced, her phone hadn't stopped ringing. Her calendar was now booked solid with potential clients.

"Knock, knock." Her cousin's voice called from the doorway.

With the phone receiver still glued to her ear, Addie waved her cousin inside. "Excellent. I will see you next Wednesday at two o'clock. I look forward to working with you."

Chloe dropped into the chair near her desk and placed a white paper bag in front of her. "I thought you might be hungry," she said when Addie hung up the phone.

"Starved. Thank you." Without any hesitation, she pulled out the mini calzone from the bag. "I haven't stopped all day."

Chloe leaned back in her chair and crossed her legs. "Business is good, I take it?"

"Good doesn't begin to explain it." She raised the calzone toward her mouth, the scent of oregano teasing her nose. "I've had more people call me since that picture appeared in the paper than all of last month."

Her cousin gave her an *I told you so* look. "And you were all upset about it. I bet you're not anymore."

Addie gave her a shrug, her mouth full of food.

"All the bakeries have had a surge in sales, too, especially the one on Benefit Street. I think people keep stopping in hoping to see Trent Sherbrooke seated at a table."

"I'd still like to know who sent that picture to the paper."

"Who cares?" Chloe asked. "You're benefiting from it and I'm sure Trent Sherbrooke is used to being in papers by now."

"I care." Addie popped another chunk of her calzone into her mouth and glanced at her watch. She had another hour before her appointment with Phyllis Harney on the East Side. When she'd worked for Ducat and Wakefield, she helped redesign the woman's gourmet kitchen. Right before the picture in the paper came out, Phyllis called and set up an appointment. Evidently, she'd divorced and wanted to redecorate her master suite.

"So what did the two of you talk about that afternoon?" Chloe asked. "You never did tell me."

The conversation with Trent rolled through her mind. "Nothing, really. I told him a little about what I did."

Her cousin leaned forward. "He looked rather happy in that picture. You must have said something to him."

"I teased him a bit about not spilling coffee on me again." Addie picked at the calzone on her desk.

Chloe shook her head, a look of pity on her face. "Seriously, Addie. You had Trent Sherbrooke sitting across from you and you made jokes? Man, don't you know how to flirt a little? If that had been me I wouldn't have been talking about coffee."

Addie rolled her eyes. Her cousin was always on the lookout for Mister Right. Hopefully one of these days she'd find him. Maybe then she'd stop pestering her about it. "It wouldn't have mattered if I flirted or not, Chloe. A man like him wouldn't be interested in me even if I stripped in front of him."

"You still could've tried." Chloe took a sip from the water bottle she'd brought in with her. "Since we are on the topic of men, did you and Dustin ever go out?"

"Yes, and there will not be a second date." Addie gathered up what she needed for her afternoon appointment.

"Why not?"

A close friend Chloe had met in a college night class, Dustin had been a nice enough guy. He just wasn't the guy for her. "He was as nice as you said, but we have nothing in common, Chloe. Besides, I don't have a lot of free time right now. Honestly, I think you and he should get together."

Chloe shook her head, her ponytail swinging back and forth. "No way. We're friends."

"So?" Addie asked, surprised by how adamantly her cousin answered.

"I don't want to mess up our friendship," she said as she checked her phone. "I need to go. I'll talk with you later."

When her cousin left, she took one more bite of her calzone and wrapped the rest up. She'd never understand her cousin. If she and Dustin were already friends, that seemed like a great start for a relationship. And after meeting Dustin and hearing him talk about her cousin, she suspected that he was already half in love with Chloe. Perhaps next time she saw Chloe she'd press the matter. She'd have to be a little subtle about it of course, but her cousin wasn't the only one that could play cupid.

FIVE

ADDIE TOOK a seat in one of the leather chairs, crossed her legs and watched as the woman behind the desk reached for the phone. Her appointment wasn't for another fifteen minutes and Shirley, the secretary behind the desk, had informed her that Mr. Sherbrooke was just finishing up a conference call and would be with her shortly.

All week she'd been both dreading and looking forward to this appointment. During her time in Boston she'd worked on projects for some wealthy clients, but she'd never been in charge. Others at the firm brought in the clients and doled out the work. Before any of her designs or ideas could even be presented to clients, her supervisors needed to approve them. This time she was on the front line. Nothing stood between her and the client. She'd started her own company for that very reason. However, in the two years since she'd started Designs by Addison, she'd never had a client of Trent Sherbrooke's stature. The idea of working for him thrilled and terrified her at the same time.

She gripped and ungripped the strap of her bag. His status as a high profile client wasn't the only thing that had her stomach in a knot. The picture from the paper remained a worry as well. While he was by no means a stranger to tabloid headlines, he may think twice before hiring her because of it. In truth, ever since the picture appeared she'd expected a phone call from his secretary canceling today's meeting.

At the sound of a door opening, Addie looked toward the office door behind Shirley's desk. "I emailed you a list of construction proposals. Please make sure they get to Sherbrooke Enterprises." When Trent finished speaking he turned his gaze on her. "Ms. Raimono, sorry to keep you waiting. Please come in."

She gripped the straps of her bag tighter and a spasm of pain shot through her hand as she stood. "No need to apologize. I was early." She walked past him into his office, the scent of his musky aftershave teasing her. Inside the office her eyes swept around the room, ideas emerging before she even sat down.

"Please have seat." Trent stopped near the conference table by the window. "As you can guess, this office wasn't decorated for me."

Addie pulled out one of the upholstered chairs at the table and sat. "No, this office was decorated for a woman. But we can change that." She reached into her bag and pulled out her laptop while Trent took the seat next to her. Then, before he could make any comments, she pulled up her standard client questionnaire. "Before I do anything else, I like to get to know more about my clients. What colors they like, types of fabrics or patterns they prefer. That sort of thing. After that, I can get measurements and input them into my design software. From there I can generate possible 3-D options for you to review."

Trent didn't respond right away. Instead, he placed his fore-arms on the table and clasped his hands together. "Ask away."

As if her eyes had a mind of their own, she looked over at his tanned hands with their long fingers and short nails. *He's just another client. Think about how you teased him the other day.*

Clearing her throat, she dragged her eyes back to the computer. "Okay, to start with what colors do you prefer?"

"Silver, red." Trent paused for a moment. "And green."

As he answered, she typed. "Can you be more specific? For example, do you prefer a darker red like crimson or more of a fire engine red? Forest green or more of a lime green?"

"I'd say more of a fire engine red and green similar to the beads in your necklace."

She glanced down at her necklace and then up again at Trent, her eyes locking with his. "Forest green," she mumbled like an idiot unable to look away from his intense eyes. A beautiful shade of sapphire blue shared by many of the Sherbrookes.

"A shade or two lighter is nice, too."

His comment reminded her they still had more questions to get through. "Okay, what colors do you dislike?" She focused on the blinking cursor on the screen.

"Yellow," he answered with no hesitation. "And that brown coffee becomes after you add cream to it."

The amusement in his voice had her looking over at him again. When she saw the smile on his face her own lips curled upward and some of her anxiety washed away. "I'll keep that in mind."

Quickly, they went through the remainder of her questions. "I'd like to get some measurements of the office now, if you don't mind." She leaned over and pulled an electric tape measure from her bag. As she straightened back up, a hand settled on her arm causing her stomach to flip flop.

"No, of course not, but before you do that I'd like to apologize."

Nothing he had said or done since the start of their meeting required an apology.

"The picture in the paper," he said as she continued to think over their meeting so far. "I don't know who sold it to the paper, but I hope it hasn't caused you any problems."

Oh, why did he have to bring that up today? The whole idea that some reporter had linked them together embarrassed her. "It shocked me, but it hasn't caused me any problems."

As he moved his hand, he gave her a smile and once again her stomach did a little shimmy. There was no mistaking why women around the world threw themselves at him. Not only did he have an overabundance of money and charm, but he was drop dead gorgeous to top it off. In many ways it struck her as unfair that one man would have so much going for him.

Holding up her electronic tape measure she pushed back her chair. "Once I get some measurements I can create some models based on your preferences."

Next to her, Trent stood as well. "Excellent. How long does that generally take?"

"It varies. Did you have a specific time frame in mind?" She crossed to the opposite side of the office to measure the width between the office door and the windows.

While she took measurements, he remained near the table, but his eyes followed her. Or at least she thought they did. The hairs on the back of her neck said they did. *You're imagining things.* While she waited for an answer, she returned to her computer and typed in the measurements.

"The sooner the better, Addison." The sound of her name in his deep sensual voice washed over her like a warm caress.

"I could have some preliminary designs for you by Friday." It would require a late night or two, but she could get it done.

"Friday, my day is booked solid until about six o'clock. Would that work for you?"

She'd have to ask Chloe to cover her shift at the bakery, but that shouldn't be a problem. She'd covered for her cousin more than enough in the past. "I'll have some ideas ready for you by then." She powered down her laptop prepared to leave.

Trent smiled. "I look forward to seeing what you come up with and perhaps we can discuss another project then."

It took all her will power to push down the excitement surging forward. He'd not even seen her work yet, but already had another project in mind. She couldn't screw this opportunity up.

"I understand you do interior design work as well as decorating," he began.

Addie nodded. "Yes, although lately I've done more decorating and staging."

"Last year I purchased a home in Newport. I'm interested in having it redesigned. If you're interested I'd like to get your ideas for it as well."

Her hands shook as she slid her laptop into her bag and she bit down on her lip to keep from blurting out an answer. While she wanted the project he proposed, she didn't want to come across as too eager.

"I'd need to see the home first, but I'd be happy to come up with some designs. I have some agreements with contractors who do fabulous work. Just so you know, a project like that involves much more than this one. There are building codes that need to be adhered to and structural attributes that come into play sometimes making certain things impossible.

Trent nodded when she finished. "When we meet on Friday we can agree on a time for you to see the house."

TRENT SAW her eyes light up the moment he mentioned his home in Newport, but much to her credit she didn't overreact. Rather, she remained polite and professional, if not a bit restrained. Perhaps a bit too restrained. He'd enjoyed her sense of humor the other day in the bakery and hoped to see more of it today. He'd tried to coax it out of her, but all he'd managed was a smile from her. He figured that made sense. This was a business meeting not a casual conversation.

With her bag packed up, she slipped its straps over her

shoulder and pushed her chair in. "I'll see you on Friday night." She crossed to the door, but he got there first and opened it for her.

"I'll walk out with you. I need to grab a quick lunch before my next meeting. Would you care to join me?" Only twelve o'clock, he figured she'd not had a chance to eat yet either.

She fiddled with the strap of her bag. "Thank you for the offer, but I have an appointment in Warwick at one."

He walked alongside her and into the elevator. "Some other time perhaps."

She gave him a small tentative smile as the elevator doors closed behind them and it began its decent. When they reached the ground floor he allowed her to exit first and then followed her outside.

"Enjoy your lunch. I'll see you on Friday," she said before heading down the sidewalk, the sun glittering off her chestnut-colored hair.

For a moment he remained in place, his eyes following her as she walked away. When she turned the corner and disappeared from view, he crossed the street toward the Indian restaurant, which, in his opinion, served the best Indian cuisine he'd tasted outside of New Delhi.

"Mr. Sherbrooke, it's so good to see you again," the restaurant owner said, his voice heavily accented. "Please follow me." The restaurant owner led him to a corner table and handed him a menu.

Trent didn't bother to look at it; he already knew what he wanted. As he waited for his waiter, he mapped out his plan for winning over Ms. Addison Raimono. From their few meetings so far he'd learned much about her. She had a witty sense of humor but strived to maintain a professional appearance. She didn't seem taken by his family name or reputation. Despite the invasion of privacy the pictures in the paper had caused, she hadn't lashed out or pointed fingers in his direction.

His instincts told him a subtler, gradual approach was the way to go with her. On Friday after their meeting he'd invite her out for dinner. That would be a good way to start his pursuit in earnest. Then he'd invite her to visit his home in Newport on Saturday or Sunday. The more time they spent in each other's company, the better.

ADDIE REACHED for the bottle of cola on her desk and took a sip. Although she preferred flavored seltzer water to cola, this afternoon she wanted the extra pick me up the caffeine and sugar would give her. The previous night she'd spent a few hours putting together the final touches on the project proposal for the Burleys and worked on the models for her meeting with Trent tonight. By the time she'd crawled into bed, the clock read three. Despite the hour, her mind refused to cooperate and turn itself off. Instead, it had raced with thoughts of her upcoming appointment with Trent. If he accepted her ideas and hired her, he'd be her first high profile client. The mere thought made her as giddy as a child on Christmas morning. But would her ideas be good enough? She'd spent hours agonizing over them, but what if he didn't like them? Then not only would she not get this project, but he'd also withdraw his offer regarding his home in Newport. While her company wouldn't collapse if she lost those projects, she knew she might never get another chance at such a client. At the same time, if he hated her designs she may never see him again. As much as she hated to admit it, that fact had just as much to do with keeping her awake. If he didn't hire her, she'd have no reason to see him again.

That's the least of your concerns. She took another sip from her drink and checked the time. If she left now, she'd get to his office five minutes early. She'd read somewhere that was an acceptable amount of time to arrive before a meeting.

After tossing the empty soda can in the trash under her desk, she grabbed her bag and headed outside. Although the weather channel claimed temperatures today were lower than yesterday, the air remained thick and muggy. The only real difference she noticed from the rest of the week was the dark clouds in the sky. The meteorologist on the morning news warned that heavy showers and thunderstorms would pass through the area tonight, and from the looks of it, she'd gotten it right. With any luck, however, the storms would hold off until she got home.

JUST AS ADDIE stepped inside the building, which housed Sherbrooke Enterprises and The Helping Hands Foundation, the first rumble of thunder filled the air stopping her in her tracks. She hated thunderstorms. As a child she'd hide whenever a storm came through. She'd grown out of that habit, but the rumble of thunder and the flashes of lightning still set her on edge.

There's nothing to be afraid of. In the elevator she pressed the button for the tenth floor and repeated the statement over in her head. Thunder was nothing more than noise caused by changes in the weather. As for the lightning, the worst that could happen was that the power would go out for a short time.

When she stepped out of the elevator and into the reception area, Trent's secretary remained at her desk, her eyes focused on her computer screen oblivious to the flashes of light outside the windows. "Excuse me. I have an appointment tonight at six o'clock."

The woman looked up at her and smiled. "Please have a seat. He's on the phone at the moment."

With no other option, Addie sat and waited, her full attention on counting the seconds between the flashes of lightning and the thunder. Although not a truly scientific method, the counting gave her a general idea of how close the storm was to her.

Judging by the sound of it, the storm was getting closer rather than farther away.

When another rumble of thunder filled the silence, the secretary looked over at her. "Looks like the news was right. It said we were in for storms this weekend. As much as I hate the rain, we need it."

Addie nodded in agreement. "It has been a dry summer."

"I just hope the rain holds off until I get home. I hate driving in it and I need new windshield wipers," the secretary said as she began to shut down her computer.

From her seat Addie glanced out the floor-to-ceiling windows. So far not a single drop of rain had fallen, but the sky warned it was just a matter of time.

The door opened behind Shirley, and Addie looked away from the window. "I'm sorry to keep you waiting. That call took longer than I expected." Trent stood in the doorway to his office. He'd rolled up the sleeves of his white dress shirt, but otherwise looked like the perfect model for corporate America.

"Please come in," he said as he took a step into the reception area and stopped next to his secretary's desk. "Shirley, have a good weekend. See you on Monday."

Shirley gathered up her belongings. "There were some last minute changes to your schedule for next week. I updated everything on your calendar, Mr. Sherbrooke."

Addie passed by Trent and entered his office but could hear Shirley as she continued to speak to him. As she waited for him to join her, she glanced around. A suit jacket matching his pants hung over the back of his desk chair. Several documents remained on his desk, as did a mug. A laptop remained open on his conference table along with several file folders.

Behind her the door clicked, causing her to glance in that direction. "Please have a seat." He gestured toward the chairs around the conference table. "I expected that call to be over in under ten minutes." He closed his laptop and moved it and the folders off to the side. "I hope you weren't waiting long."

Taking the seat facing the door, Addie pulled out her own laptop. "I just got here," she reassured him. "Now, I have two different proposals for you today. Please keep in mind that I can make changes to either of them or start over altogether." She logged into her computer and brought up the files containing her plans for Trent's office. "I tried to keep with more traditional materials but at the same time keep the look masculine and contemporary. At least in my opinion, often when a decorator strives for a more contemporary atmosphere it becomes too feminine." Her body sensed his proximity as he took the seat next to her.

"Sounds like you're describing my father's office since he let my stepmother redecorate."

"It can be hard to find that right balance. Anyway, this is my first proposal." She turned the laptop so he could see the screen better. "I picked a dove gray for the walls. It's light enough to go with any other colors in the office but gives the walls just enough color, Mr. Sherbrooke." In her personal opinion, anything was better than the peachy beige that covered the walls now. "And I found a carpet a few shades darker that would complement the color."

Trent pulled the laptop closer to him, his arm brushing against hers. As if struck by the lightning outside, she pulled her arm away and hoped the heat she felt didn't show on her face. "I kept this conference table but replaced the chairs. The ones you see are in forest green, but they also come in black as well as brown. I replaced the desk with a larger ebony-colored one, but if you prefer something lighter I found a similar one in a nice shade of walnut." Addie went through everything in her proposal explaining what she'd chosen. Next to her, Trent remained silent, not giving her any hint of his thoughts on her ideas. By the time she finished, her mouth was dry and a tangle of nerves sat in her stomach.

"Like I said, Mr. Sherbrooke, this is just a preliminary idea. Anything can be adjusted or changed." Under the table her fingers drummed against her thigh.

"Please, call me Trent."

Trent transferred his gaze from the screen to her, meeting her eyes as another flash of lightning filled the room. Unable to stop herself, Addie flinched and took a deep breath. The storm was getting closer.

"Are you okay?"

She heard the concern in his voice and pasted on a smile. "Fine. Just not a huge fan of thunderstorms." She reached for the computer, prepared to bring up her second proposal for his office. "I have another proposal if you'd rather see that one."

"No need. I like this. How long will it take to get it all done?"

Addie blinked as his words sunk in. "Once work begins it shouldn't take long. I have a painter and a floor company that I work with. I can call them tomorrow and schedule them. I already checked with the manufacturers and the furniture can be here in two weeks." At first they'd claimed a month, but when she'd informed them the furniture was for a Sherbrooke, they'd changed their tune.

"Excellent. Send any invoices to my secretary and she'll take care of them. And if you have a contract prepared already, I'll sign it tonight."

She pressed her lips together to keep the smile that wanted to break free hidden. "I do have a copy of my standard agreement." She reached for her bag and the folder inside. "As soon as I have everything arranged I will let your secretary know." She passed the agreement to him. Although short, it contained all pertinent information and protected her and her business.

"At our last meeting I mentioned my home in Newport. If

you're interested, I'd like to arrange a time for you to see it."
Trent read the contract as he spoke.

Now that was a stupid question if she'd ever heard one. "Just
let me know what works for you."

Trent scrawled his name on the contract and then grabbed his
phone. "This weekend is open for me. Does either day work for
you?"

"Saturday I am free." In order to get Chloe to cover her
Friday night shift she'd promised to cover her cousin's shift on
Sunday.

"Saturday it is then." He handed the papers back to her. "If
you'd like I can pick you up and we can drive down together. I
know I wouldn't mind the company."

More thunder rumbled outside, but Addie feared he'd still
heard the excited thud of her heartbeat. "Only if it doesn't incon-
venience you. I don't mind driving down."

Trent gave her a smile that used his entire face. No wonder
he had such a reputation as an international playboy. His smile
alone would send women right to him.

THE SLIGHTEST HINT of color already on her cheeks dark-
ened and she swallowed. Throughout their meeting she'd yet
again remained professional if not a bit nervous. Before this
moment, he'd wondered if perhaps he shouldn't pressure her. At
least during this and their previous meetings she'd displayed no
outward signs that she was attracted to him. She hadn't flirted or
done any of the typical things women tried to snag him. But then
she'd blushed when his hand came into contact with hers and
it'd grown darker when he offered to pick her up.

"The company would be nice. Does eleven o'clock work for
you?" His original reason for asking her to stop by tonight rather
than sometime next week was because he planned to ask her out
for dinner after their meeting. Now though, he rethought his

strategy. Tomorrow after they toured his house, he'd take her out. Once she left tonight he'd make reservations for them at the Spiced Pear. As much as he wanted to proceed with the plan he and Marty agreed on, he didn't want to come on too strong and spook Addison away either.

"Uh, sure. That time works." She pulled out a business card and wrote on the back. "Here is my address, but if you need to call me, my cell number is on the front."

He accepted the card even though he didn't need it. Thanks to Marty he had her home address, as well as the address of her parents, already in his desk. "Great. If you want to wait a moment, I'll walk out with you. I'm going to call it a day."

Before she answered, he stood and walked back to his desk. Grabbing his suit jacket, his eyes followed Addie as she packed up her own belongings. With deliberate movements she placed one item in at a time as if each thing had a specific place. When she finished, she stood, smoothed down her dress and then slipped the strap of her bag over her right shoulder. Unlike the previous times they'd met, she wore a dress tonight, and the sleeveless style revealed her well-toned upper arms.

"All set?" he asked as he retrieved his briefcase and came around toward the door.

Rather than speak, she nodded and walked toward the door. On cue, he pulled it open and allowed her to exit first. Not that he minded in the least. With her in front of him, he could let his eyes wander and appreciate her form without her any the wiser. And he definitely liked what he saw. She was an average height, but she had killer legs, perfectly shaped and toned. He suspected she exercised on a regular basis. Her waist was tiny and although she had her back to him now, he already had a mental picture of her breasts. Judging by the way her dress fit, they were lush and full but not ridiculously large.

When they reached the elevator, he pushed the button. "Please dress casually tomorrow. Whatever you normally wear on the weekend," he said as a way to break the silence. "I certainly won't be wearing a tie."

Addie laughed, a sweet lyrical sound. "Then I might still be in my pj's when you pick me up."

The image of the type of sleepwear worn by the women he usually spent time with popped up. While he had no doubt Addie would look fantastic in any of those outfits, he doubted those were the type of pj's she wore. "Whatever works for you," he answered as the elevator door opened and they stepped inside.

"So where in Newport is your home? Is it on Bellevue Avenue?"

Slowly the elevator began its descent and he leaned up against the glass wall. "No. It's on Ocean Avenue. It was built —" The loud crack of lightning echoed through the elevator, cutting off Trent's sentence just before the lights blinked and then went out.

"Please tell me we're not stuck." Addison's voice trembled from the other side of the glass elevator.

He remembered her reaction to the storm in his office. "It shouldn't take them long to get us going again." Stepping forward, he picked up the emergency phone in the elevator wall. After a few seconds, a voice responded on the other end.

"Security."

"This is Trent Sherbrooke. How long until the power is restored? I'm stuck in the elevator with a business associate."

"I'm not sure, Mr. Sherbrooke. The entire block is out. Maintenance is trying to contact the electric company. It may be a while."

"Bad news?" Addie asked when he hung up the phone. She stood near the back wall, her arms crossed just above her waist.

"The whole block is out." He placed his briefcase on the floor along with his suit jacket. In the distance he heard the hint of thunder or at least he assumed that was it. "They know we're in here and are working on the problem."

"Last winter an ice storm took out all the power in the city. It took them days to get everyone up again," she said with the barest hint of a catch in her voice.

He'd spent the worst of the winter months in England working on a land acquisition project so he'd not been affected. "I'm sure it won't take them that long to get us out."

"I'm sure you're right," Addie answered. Thanks to the security lights in the elevator he could see her face and her facial expression revealed her true feelings on the matter.

In a few short steps he crossed to her. "Like I was saying, my house was built in 1911 for Madeline Curran. Her father made his fortune in the shipping business and the house was a wedding present to her," he explained as a way to distract her.

Outside, a streak of lightning lit up the sky, followed soon after by a distant clap of thunder.

"Sounds like the storm is moving away." Addie moved next to him, her arm bumping up against his.

"Counting the seconds between the flash and the sound? I do that sometimes, too."

"Knowing how close or far away it is helps," she said. "Too bad it hasn't rained yet. We could use it. My mom has complained all summer about her grass not getting enough water. She's a bit obsessed with her yard. She loves to garden. Her roses are her pride and joy."

Trent latched onto the everyday topic. "What about you? Do you enjoy gardening as well?"

"I kill everything I try to grow. I once even managed to kill a cactus," she said with a hint of humor in her voice.

He looked over at her profile. "How did you manage that? I thought those were easy." Plants weren't his thing, although he knew a great deal about them thanks to his mom. His mom had adored flowers. She'd had a whole greenhouse full of beautiful plants at their estate on Martha's Vineyard when he was a child.

His father's second wife had cleared the entire thing out not long after they married.

Addie dropped her arms to her sides. "So did I, but I overwatered it. Now the only time I have flowers, they come from the florist in a vase or they are made of silk."

With no idea how long they might be stuck, Trent lowered himself to the floor, his long legs stretched out in front of him. Then he took his suit jacket and spread it out next to him. "You might want to get comfortable. Or as comfortable as possible." He gestured to the suit jacket he'd spread out. "Have a seat."

"You probably don't want to use your jacket like that."

She looked down at him as she spoke and for a moment he couldn't look away from her eyes. A blue much lighter than his own, they reminded him of the oceans off of Hawaii. "I'm not worried about it."

Addie didn't offer any further argument. Instead, she lowered herself to the floor, then smoothed down her dress. "Okay, but I'm not paying for the dry cleaning," she said in a playful tone.

"Fair enough," he said with a laugh. "So if you weren't stuck in here with me what would you be doing tonight?" As he spoke, he tried to ignore the hunger pains in his stomach.

Her shoulders brushed against his as she shrugged and clasped her hands in her lap. "Depends. Sometimes I work on contracts. Other times I help out at the bakery."

Although he knew she wasn't involved with anyone at the moment, thanks to Marty, he'd expected a different answer. Most people he knew their age devoted their weekends to pleasure. Then again, most of the people he associated with had few responsibilities to begin with.

"What about you?" she asked as she turned her face toward him. "Actually, never mind. Forget I asked that."

"Why? I just asked you the same question."

"It was an inappropriate question to ask a client." Her voice took on a more formal tone, indicating she'd forgotten at least for a moment that he'd hired her for a job.

"Trust me, it doesn't bother me. You may not have noticed, but my social life is often public knowledge." His stomach growled again. This time so loud the security guards on the first floor probably heard it.

"Hungry?" Addie asked, reaching into her bag.

"What gave it away?"

"I figured it was either that or the thunder is getting closer again," she teased, her voice losing some of its formality again. "Here, this should help." She handed him a high protein bar. "I have two more in my bag if you want them."

He accepted the snack and tore it open without even looking at the flavor. "Thanks. Do you always prepare for being stuck in elevators?"

Next to him, she pulled out a bottle of water. "I started keeping snacks in my bag when I worked in Boston. Sometimes traffic would be so bad it would take me forever to get home and I'd often get hungry."

He bit into the dense chocolate-covered bar. Though not at all how he planned to spend his night, getting stuck in the elevator with Addie was proving beneficial. It allowed him the perfect opportunity to learn more about her. "You commuted into Boston every day from Rhode Island?"

Addie licked a drop of water from her bottom lip and Trent's eyes followed its path. Once again he noticed how plump and full her lips were. In fact, he could imagine just how they'd feel against his.

"No, when I worked in Boston I shared an apartment with a friend in Marlborough. I moved to Cumberland when I started work in Providence."

Overhead, the lights blinked a few times; then after the third time they remained on. "Finally," Addie said, the relief in her voice audible.

Trent stood and reached down to help Addie to her feet. "I apologize if I made such terrible company." He infused some humor into his voice, but judging by her straight face, she'd missed it.

"No, not at all." She slipped her hand into his and allowed him to help her up. "Stuck in here with no power—"

His mouth curved into a smile. "I was kidding, Addie." Before then he'd used her full name but recalled that her family called her Addie for short. Using the nickname now gave the situation a touch more intimacy. He took a step closer. "I'm glad the power is on again, too, although I enjoyed our conversation." He contemplated kissing her. To fulfill Marty's timetable he needed to push things forward. And he'd been known to kiss women he'd known even less time than Addie. Hell, he'd made love to women he'd known less time than her. Even so, he held back. Not because his mouth didn't ache to taste her, but because she was different from women he spent time with. If he kissed her now, who knew how she might respond?

The elevator stopped and chimed just before the door behind him opened. "Looks like we made it," Addie said, her voice soft and clear as she held out his suit jacket, which she'd picked up from the floor.

Releasing her other hand, he accepted the jacket and then grabbed his briefcase from the floor. "After you."

In silence they exited the elevator and crossed the main lobby to the glass doors. Outside only a handful of vehicles passed by as most people had already left the city prepared to put the workweek behind them.

"Looks like leaving the city should be easy tonight," Addie remarked as they stood outside.

"Let me walk you to your car." Although the storm had passed, the night sky remained darker than normal for the time of day.

Addie took a step away from him. "I'll be fine. I'm just in the garage around the corner."

"Me, too." He moved forward so that once again they stood less than an arm's length apart.

It took only a matter of minutes for them to get from Trent's building to the garage and the third level. "I'll see you tomorrow." Addie stopped next to a white Toyota but made no attempt to get in. "If it's easier for you I can meet you in Newport." She finally opened her trunk and deposited her bag inside.

Not on your life. A car ride together to and from Newport would provide him with the perfect opportunity to further Marty's plan. "I'm looking forward to the company." He pulled open her car door.

Addie stepped into her car. "Okay. See you tomorrow," she said before she closed the car door.

Trent watched until the taillights disappeared around the corner; then he took the stairs to the lower gated level where he'd parked.

SIX

No, that doesn't look right either. She looked ready for Easter dinner. Addie pulled the dress over her head and tossed it on the bed. Already a small pile of outfits covered the mossy green bedspread. Not many options remained in her closet. She'd already pushed aside her typical business clothes. He'd told her to dress casually. But casual for her meant cut offs and a tank top. She couldn't meet with a client dressed like that no matter what he said.

"What happened in here?" Chloe asked. She'd stopped by before breakfast to use her laptop for a paper because her apartment had not regained power yet.

Addie pushed aside the dress she'd worn to a cousin's graduation. "I'm meeting with a client today, and nothing seems right."

Chloe pushed the clothes closer to the center of the bed and sat. "Must be some client. I've never seen you worry this much about dressing for your clients."

Without responding, she grabbed a lilac colored skirt from a hanger. If she paired it with a white tank top and wore her white silk blouse over it she might be casual enough while still maintaining the look of a professional. Pulling the tank top from its hanger she held it and the skirt up against her body and turned. "What do you think if I wear this and add my white blouse? You know the one I usually just knot in the front?"

Chloe leaned down and scooped up a top from the floor. "It'll look fine. So who's this client anyway? Must be someone important for you to get this crazy about how you look."

She'd never overthought how she looked for a client. As long as she appeared professional, a blue skirt was just as good as the gray one next to it. But today no matter how hard she tried, she couldn't lump Trent in with her usual clients and not just because of his bank account and good looks. When she was near him, a million butterflies took flight in her stomach and she found it hard to sit still. She once again felt like she did when she'd been a freshman in high school and Ben Smith, a senior, tutored her in science. Every time she met Ben at the library for a study session, she turned into a bumbling mass of nerves that could put no more than two words together. She'd been both relieved and disappointed when the school year ended and Ben graduated. Since then no guy had made her feel like that again. At least not until now.

After she slipped on her clothes, Addie pulled open the window blind and took a quick glimpse outside. "Was that car out there when you got here?" she asked, her gaze on the small black sedan parked across the street.

"The black Honda?" Chloe asked, as she slipped hangers into Addie's discarded clothes. "Yup. I figured they were visiting that nosy neighbor of yours across the way. Why?"

Addie turned her back on the window. Her cousin was probably right. Just because she'd only seen the car around this week didn't mean it wasn't a friend of Beverly's. "Just curious." Despite her dismissive answer, she couldn't shake her unease. Not once had she seen anyone go into or come out of Beverly's house that week except Beverly herself.

"How's the paper coming along? You haven't done much work since you've been here."

"Once you leave I'll finish it. So you never answered me. Who's this client you're meeting this afternoon?"

Outside a car door closed and a moment later her doorbell rang. Without answering her cousin, Addie crossed the room and went downstairs. Before she reached the door she took a slow measured breath. *He's just a client, nothing more, nothing less.*

The moment she opened the door the swarm of butterflies in her stomach multiplied and grew some extra long wings. Holy wow. Dressed in a suit and seated in his office he'd looked fabulous. The very image of power and wealth wrapped up in a handsome package. Today though, in khaki pants and a short-sleeved blue and white-striped polo shirt with his sunglasses dangling from the front and the sun dancing across his dirty blond hair, he looked godlike.

"I'm a few minutes early. It didn't take me as long as I thought to get here. I hope that's okay," he said, the first to speak.

Addie took a step back so he could enter. "Not a problem. Please come in. I just need to grab my things and we can go."

She took another step back and bumped into a body. "Chloe, sorry," she said as she glanced over her shoulder.

"No biggie." She pinched Addie in the back, a clear signal she wanted an introduction.

"Trent, this is my cousin, Chloe." She nodded in her cousin's direction. "Chloe, this is Trent Sherbrooke. I'm redecorating his office and perhaps his house in Newport." Addie stepped away from her cousin. "I'll be right back." She retreated up the stairs, leaving Chloe and Trent to exchange pleasantries while she grabbed her things. Once in the safety of her room, she glanced one final time in her mirror and grabbed her bag with her laptop and her purse, then returned to the front door. "I'm ready." She walked past her cousin. "If you need any extra paper for the printer, it's in the bottom drawer of my desk."

"Thanks. See you later."

In silence she descended the stairs and started down the walkway, but before she reached the car she stopped when she thought she saw someone or something move inside the sedan across the street. *It's just a shadow.* A person would be nuts to sit in a parked car on a day like this. Already the thermometer on her tiny deck read ninety-five and that didn't take into account the humidity.

Next to her Trent pulled open the door to a silver Mercedes with heavily tinted windows. Without a word she sat, the leather soft and warm against her legs. Unable to help herself, her eyes followed Trent as he crossed in front of the car and then slid behind the steering wheel.

"You look surprised. Is something wrong?"

Addie folded her hands in her lap. "No, I just... well, I expected something else."

"I like to use this sometimes because it draws less attention than my other ones."

His answer reminded her again just who sat behind the wheel next to her.

"The controls for your seat are right here." He pointed to some dials near the glove box. "You can make the seat as warm or cool as you want. The dial all the way to the right controls the lumbar massage in your seat." He started the car, but kept it in neutral. "You can also control the air temperature on your side." He pointed to another dial above the stereo controls. "Please make yourself comfortable." Checking the rearview mirror, he put the car in reverse and backed into the street.

"I could get used to a massage every time I drive."

The corner of Trent's mouth inched up. "It's a nice feature for longer drives."

Once underway, she grabbed onto the only topic they had to

discuss: his office. "So I ordered the office furniture last night. The distributor promised it in two weeks. And I left a message with my painter. I expect to hear back from him today or tomorrow."

"Excellent. I'm eager to have it done." Trent merged onto the highway, then dropped the car into fifth gear.

"I've been looking forward to this since last night." Addie grimaced when she realized how her statement must sound, and heat warmed the back of her neck. "That didn't come out right," she said as a way to clarify her statement. "I meant I've been looking forward to seeing your home. This morning I did some research on the property and found a few older photos but nothing recent."

From the driver's seat Trent sighed and looked over at her for a moment. "And for a second I thought you liked my company. I should've known."

Wonderful, not only do I look like an idiot but I insulted him, too. "It's not that. I do but—"

A deep rich chuckle filled the car. "I'm giving you a hard time, Addie. Relax. You look about ready to jump out."

In front of them a minivan cut them off without using a directional and Trent swore his voice barely audible.

"I hate when people do that," she said, grateful the other car had distracted him from their conversation.

"You and me both." Trent reached out to adjust the temperature on his side of the car. "So does your cousin live with you?" he asked, starting up another conversation.

TRENT STOPPED the car in front of the three-story mansion. From the outside it looked pristine, nothing like it had during his last visit more than a year ago. Thanks to the maintenance company he'd hired, the exterior received regular maintenance now. He assumed the inside looked just as flawless. After updating Marty on the situation, he'd hired a service to come in and clean the interior from top to bottom in anticipation for Addie's visit.

Salty ocean air washed over him when he got out of his car and he paused for a moment just to savor it. There was just something about the air near the ocean. It brought back memories of his childhood long before his mom died, when he'd run around Cliff House with his brothers and cousins or visit Martha's Vineyard and spend hours outside while his mom tended her flowers.

"It looks like you've already done work here," Addie said when he opened the car door for her. "In the pictures I saw the house looked a little run-down and the grounds overgrown."

The house's exterior had suffered from years of neglect, which was most likely why it had been on the market for several years before he purchased it the year before. "I had all the exterior projects completed last summer, but went overseas before anything could be done inside." He led her up the front steps and unlocked the door. "After you."

A quick glance around the entryway showed that the maid service he'd hired had done a fabulous job. Sunlight from the windows gleamed off the polished wood as well as the granite tiles. Not a single cobweb or speck of dust showed on the light fixtures and the barest scent of sandalwood permeated the air.

"Do you have any idea what you'd like done?" Next to him, Addie looked around the empty space.

"Not a one. Honestly, this is the first time I've been in here since I bought it." He held a hand out toward her. "Why don't we take a tour and then come up with some ideas."

It took a second or two before she accepted his hand. "You haven't spent any time here?"

In the past year he hadn't stepped foot in this house or the condo he owned in Aspen, but he kept that to himself. While she knew exactly who he was, he didn't want to reinforce the differences between them. Doing that could backfire on him and ruin his plans before he even got started. "My previous job required a lot of travel." Before he'd accepted his current position within Sherbrooke Enterprises, he'd spent only a handful of weeks in the US. With his hand still wrapped around hers, he led her to what had once been a library.

A large fireplace with an intricately carved mantel, a large gilded mirror above it, filled the far wall. Built in bookcases, which stretched from the floor to the ceiling, filled two of the walls while windows facing the manicured lawns took up the last one.

"Other than furniture, I wouldn't touch this room." Addie pulled her hand away and stepped closer to the fireplace. "It's gorgeous just the way it is."

He agreed. The room held a classic beauty that time hadn't ruined. "I think you're right. Let's see what else we have down here." He took her hand again and led her across the room.

Hand in hand, they went through every room on the first floor and then headed up the stairs. "In the description I read, it stated that the house contained separate his and her suites," Addie said as they entered the first of the large second-floor bedrooms. Light pink silk wall coverings lined the walls and all the woodwork was painted white. "This must have been for the wife." She released his hand and walked toward the full-length mirror mounted on the wall. "It mentioned that the door leading to the bathroom is hidden behind a mirror. This must be the one."

"You know more about this place than me." Trent's eyes followed her every move as she searched for the latch behind the mirror.

"I like to know all I can before I start a project." Her hand stopped; then she leaned closer to the space behind the mirror. "Found it." Addie looked over her shoulder at him, a triumphant smile on her face. "There's a small release right here."

From where he stood he saw nothing. "Let's see what's on the other side." He crossed the room and when she pushed on the small release the door swung open.

Light from the bedroom spilled into the hidden bathroom. Unlike the rest of the house, dust covered the built-in makeup table, and the mirror mounted on the wall contained a thin layer of dirt from years of neglect. A large claw-foot bathtub sat in one corner of the room while a pocket door remained partially open revealing a toilet in its own private space.

"This is fantastic. I love these old tubs." She paused next to it. "When you remodel this room you have to keep this tub."

The old fashion tub did add a certain charm to the room. Without even trying, he could picture Addie soaking in it, her hair draped over the back and bubbles all around her body.

"You're the expert here. If you say it needs to stay, then it stays."

Addie moved away from the tub and pulled open another door in the wall revealing a long closet. "Unless you knew about this room, you'd never guess it was here." She pulled the chain hanging from the ceiling and the overhead light switched on. "If what I read is correct, this closet will lead us to the bathroom in the husband's suite."

Trent followed her further into the closet and past the shelves to the door at the end. Coming up behind her, he reached around her and opened the door before she could. Sure enough, the door led them into a masculine version of the room they'd just left. It even contained an identical tub.

"You really didn't know about this?" she asked, looking back at him.

"No. I bought it with the assumption I'd gut most of the interior, so I did only a quick tour before I made my offer and I never opened the original plans they gave me. I brought them with me today. I thought maybe you'd find them useful."

"You can't gut this house. It has too much character." Alarm echoed in her voice. "Sure it needs some updates and a few changes here and there, but it would be a shame if you got rid of everything."

Now that he'd taken his time and gone through the home, he agreed with Addie's assessment. The home contained too much classic elegance to scrap everything. Taking Addie by the elbow, he led her toward a door he assumed would bring them into the bedroom.

"Why don't we finish our tour? Then discuss your thoughts over dinner."

"Sounds like a plan to me. I already have a few ideas in mind."

Unlike on his last visit, Trent took his time exploring the second floor with Addie. In addition to his and her suites, the second floor also contained three guest bedrooms, a bedroom that had once been a nursery judging by the mural painted on the ceiling, a small office and access to a balcony that ran the entire length of the house, providing an unobstructed view of the ocean.

"I could stand out here all day and look at this view," Addie said as they both stood at the railing looking out at the rolling waves that crashed onto the small strip of beach at the end of Trent's property.

"Do you like the beach?" He turned away from the ocean view, more interested in the way the breeze played with Addie's hair than the waves.

"It's okay. I don't spend a lot of time there, but this view is unbelievable. I wish I had my sketch book with me."

The wind blew several strands of her hair across her face. Before she could react, he reached out and tucked them back behind her ear, the back of his fingers brushing against her cheek. At the contact Addie turned away from the view and met his eyes.

"You draw?" he asked as she kept her gaze locked on his rather than turn back to the ocean.

"It's kind of like a hobby. Some people knit, I draw and paint." Once again the breeze blew some of her hair toward her face. This time before he could react, she pulled all her hair back in a ponytail and held it in place. "I should have tied my hair up today. I didn't consider how breezy it might be near the water."

"Why don't we go inside and check out the third floor? Then we can have some dinner before we head back to your house."

SITUATED at the beginning of Newport's famous cliff walk, The Spiced Pear remained a popular five star restaurant that welcomed anyone who could afford its pricey meals. Over the years, he'd taken a few women to the exclusive restaurant partially because it provided its clients with privacy. Members of the paparazzi never made it past the front entrance thanks to security guards stationed near the valet parking stand. But the privacy of the restaurant wasn't the main reason he'd picked it tonight. Instead, its romantic atmosphere had been first and foremost on his mind when he'd made the reservation.

"It is nice to see you again, Mr. Sherbrooke," the maître d' greeted when they walked inside. "If you'll please follow me, I'll show you to your table."

Placing a hand at the small of Addie's back, he followed the maître d' into the main dining room. Although on the early side, several couples sat at tables, already enjoying drinks while they waited for their dinners.

"I hope this table is satisfactory." The maître d' stopped at a table near the windows overlooking the Cliff Walk. A single candle sat in the center of the table and a red rose had been placed in front of one chair.

"Perfect, Pierre. Thank you." Before the other man could do so, he pulled out a chair for Addie and gestured for her to sit.

"Your waiter, Allen, will be right over."

With a slight nod, Trent took the seat across from Addie. "Is something wrong?" Uncertainty clouded her expression as her eyes darted around the restaurant.

When he spoke, her eyes swung toward him. "When you said dinner I thought you meant one of the restaurants on Thames Street, not here."

Trent let his forearm rest on the edge of the table. "The Spiced Pear is my favorite restaurant in Newport, but if you'd prefer somewhere else we can go."

Addie's eyes swept across the room one more time. "No, this is fine."

Her feeling uncomfortable here hadn't crossed his mind, but evidently it should have. *Time for a distraction.* "What are your initial thoughts for the house?"

Across the table, she took a sip from the water glass she'd just picked up. "I know you had other ideas, but in some of the rooms I wouldn't do anything more than redecorate." She placed the glass back on the table, but her fingers remained on the stem. "The house contains a lot of character. I think it would be a shame to tear it apart. That said, there are some areas where I'd make major design changes, starting with the kitchen. Its layout may have made sense in the 1900's but it's poorly laid out for today. There is a lot we can do in there."

Even as a person who spent little time in the kitchen, he'd noticed the antiquated design. "I agree with you. Any other thoughts?"

"The bathrooms. Although I wouldn't change everything. The clawed-foot tub and built-in makeup table in the woman's master must stay, but I'd include a shower stall and additional cabinets. I'd leave the connecting closet to the other bathroom but reduce the number of shelves so it's not so narrow."

As the evening progressed and they enjoyed dinner, Addie went through each room, listing what she believed needed to remain and what needed to be changed. With each suggestions she made, she listed her reasons, demonstrating just how well educated she was on the matter.

"You're the client, so if you want me to do some designs for the entire home I will, but I believe it'd be wrong to destroy what you already have."

He speared the final piece of tenderloin on his plate. After his tour of the home that afternoon, he'd noticed many fine details that he'd missed on his previous walk-through. "I agree with you. Can you start on designs for the kitchen and bathrooms and at the same time come up with less drastic changes for the rest of the house?"

Addie blinked a few times as realization dawned on her face. He was offering her an opportunity at a million-dollar project, and she knew it. "Yes." Her voice resonated with excitement. "I'll need proper measurements and a few ideas of what you may have in mind, but I can start right away otherwise."

Much like a current of electricity, Addie's excitement traveled across the table and zapped him. "Like I said, I have the original architectural plans with me. You're welcome to them. If they're not sufficient we can head back to the house after dinner."

Across from him, she placed her fork down beside her plate. "I'll take the plans, but if you don't mind I'd like to go back and get some photographs as well."

By the time they walked into his home again, the sun had begun to set, casting shadows across the main entryway. "Let's start in the kitchen since that's the room that requires the most work. Then if I don't finish before it gets dark I can come back and get more pictures later."

"You're the expert here. Start wherever you want and I'll follow."

With no further encouragement, she headed for the rear of the home. Inside the kitchen, she switched on the overhead lights, then began to snap pictures from various spots in the large room. In an effort to stay out of her way, he remained in a doorway, his shoulders against the frame.

"Do you want a kitchen designed for a staff or one where you would sit and eat meals you prepared yourself?" She lowered her camera and looked in his direction.

"Maybe something that could lend itself to both. I don't cook much myself, but that could change. What about you? Do you enjoy cooking?" If everything worked out as planned, any changes he made here would affect her as well.

Addie moved to the opposite end of the room and snapped another picture. "I do, but I don't do it much. Sometimes it is hard to scale down certain recipes for just one person. When I lived at home though, I used to help my mom in the kitchen all the time." She looked around the kitchen one more time. "I think I have enough pictures from in here. I'd like to get the bathrooms next."

Trent tucked away the extra tidbit of information and took her hand. "Let's head upstairs then."

In no time Addie snapped pictures of the rooms they'd agreed needed the most work and he led her back outside to his car and headed for her home.

SEVEN

ADDIE CONCLUDED her conversation with the flooring company and hung up the phone. With the start date settled on, she turned back to her computer and typed up a short email with all the final details. She hit send just as a knock sounded on her office door. Seconds later Tara entered, closed the door behind her, and then rushed to her desk her eyes wide.

"Oh my God, Addison. Trent Sherbrooke is here to see you." Tara sounded as if she'd just run a race.

"Now?" They didn't have any meetings scheduled. She'd promised to set something up with his secretary once she finished some preliminary plans for him. At the moment her designs weren't even half done.

"Yes! And God he's even more gorgeous in person than in pictures. Do you know why he's here?"

With all the extra work as of late, she'd never told Tara about the projects he'd hired her for. "I'm working on his office here in Providence and his home in Newport." That answered Tara's question but not her own. What brought him to her office today? "You can send him in, Tara."

As Tara disappeared to deliver her message, Addie glanced

around her own office. While well organized and functional it looked shabby compared to Trent's. She'd purchased much of the furniture from a local office supply store. The pictures on the walls were a combination of her own photos and paintings she'd completed over the years.

He's not here to assess my office. She turned back to her computer and pulled up what she'd put together so far. His unexpected visit must have something to do with one of his projects.

"I hope you don't mind that I just stopped in." Trent's voice cascaded over her and kicked her pulse up a notch or two.

"No, not at all. Is there a problem with the work on your office?" Unless something had gone wrong the painter should have showed up at his office that morning.

With relaxed confidence, Trent dropped into the chair across from her desk resting his ankle on his knee. "No problems. I was in the neighborhood and I thought I'd stop in."

"You were at Ambrosia again, weren't you?" She eyed him with a bit of suspicion. The bakery was just down the street and she recalled his comments from the afternoon they'd first had coffee together.

Trent shook his head. "I had a meeting with my father. But now that you mention it, I could use a cannoli and an espresso. What do you say? Care to join me?"

Addie didn't hesitate to answer. "Love to. I haven't left my desk since I came in this morning."

"Let's go then," Trent said, as he stood.

After a short stop by Tara's desk to let her know she was leaving, Addie and Trent walked down the flight of stairs to the first floor of the historical building and outside. Much like the week before, temperatures remained in the high nineties. Even with the oppressive weather, Addie turned her face toward the sky as the sunlight beat down on her. After an entire day closed up inside, the natural sunlight revived her.

For a few minutes they walked in silence, but as they

approached the courthouse, she looked over at him. "Your father's a Supreme Court Judge?" She remembered reading that Mark Sherbrooke was a judge and since the Supreme Court house wasn't far from her office it seemed like a safe guess.

"He's the Chief Justice here in Rhode Island. He has been for a while now." A messenger on a bicycle came towards them and Trent moved closer to her, giving the rider more room to pass. When he did, his shirtsleeve brushed against her arm. Unlike their outing in Newport, he again looked like the well-polished business executive in a pair of dark blue dress pants, a crisp white dress shirt and a striped tie. Even in her light skirt and short-sleeved blouse the sweat trickled down her back, so he must've been hot. Yet, despite that fact, he appeared comfortable and didn't complain.

"Your father is a Chief Justice and your uncle is the President —there must be some interesting political discussions at your family get-togethers." Addie reached for the door into the bakery, but Trent beat her to it and pulled it open for her.

Following her inside, he placed a hand on her lower back and guided her toward an empty table. "It's not too bad. My father and uncle share similar views on most topics."

As if he'd done it a thousand times before for her, he pulled a chair out for her. "Have a seat. I'll order for us. What would you like?"

She scanned the specials list posted on top of the display case. Each day her uncle featured a special pastry and sandwich. Judging by the case, they'd already sold out of the Angel Wings listed as today's special. "I'll have a biscotti and a coffee." She pulled a five-dollar bill from her wallet and held it out to him.

Trent made no move to accept the money she held out. "I got this. You can get it next time."

Before she could respond, he walked away. Get it next time? Had his statement been one to simply placate her or had he been referring to when they meet to review her designs for the house?

Her thoughts leaned toward the placating route. When they met again to review her design ideas their meeting would be held at one of their offices, not in the middle of the busy downtown bakery. Whatever his true intentions, she planned on returning the favor even if that meant bringing something to their next meeting. After all, she should be purchasing something for her client, not the other way around.

With the lunch rush over, only a handful of customers remained in the bakery. While she waited for Trent to return, she scanned the people seated, trying to determine their backstory. It was either that or stare at Trent like a teenager with her first crush while he stood at the counter and placed their order.

Tucked in at a corner table three young men sat drinking coffee. Judging by their age, style of dress and the textbooks open in front of them, she assumed they were students at Brown University. Though not the only university in the area, something about them pointed her in that direction. Across from the students, a man in a pinstripe suit sat with a cell phone glued to his ear and a half-eaten sandwich next to his open briefcase. She tagged him as a lawyer. Perhaps he'd spent the earlier part of the day at the courthouse and stopped in the bakery on his way back to his office. Addie turned her eyes to the last occupied table where two teenage girls around seventeen or so sat texting away on their phones; how they managed to type a coherent message was beyond her. Rather than being focused on the screens in front of them, their eyes remained on Trent as their fingers flew across the letters on their screens.

"They're brewing a new pot of coffee." Trent placed their afternoon snack on the table. "They promised to let us know when it is ready." Before she could move a muscle, he placed a biscotti in front of her.

"That's not a surprise. They're probably just recovering from today's lunch rush. It can get a little wild in here sometimes, and it can be hard to keep up."

Across from her, he lifted his own cup of espresso toward his mouth. "Sounds like you speak from experience."

Maintain eye contact. Don't look at his lips or think about how they'd feel against yours. "I worked here and at the bakery on Federal Hill all through high school just like everyone else in the family. Even when I was in college, I worked at one of the bakeries in the summer. It was sort of expected."

"I know how that can be." He put his cup on the table, once again giving her an unobstructed view of his mouth.

The night before she'd dreamed of him. They'd been standing on the balcony that ran the length of his home in Newport and he'd been trailing kisses down her neck.

"Everyone, even my cousin Jake, who my Uncle Warren had to drag into the office, did an internship at Sherbrooke Enterprises. Both my father and uncle insisted we know the inner workings of the company."

An image of the former playboy, Jake Sherbrooke, being dragged into an office formed and laughter bubbled up inside her. "Now that's a picture I wish the media had printed."

Trent chuckled. "It is too bad they didn't get one. What about you? Did you mind working for the family business?"

"No not really. My brother Tom hated it. Only lasted one summer before my mom banned him from ever entering the kitchen again."

"Banned him? Sounds a bit harsh. What did he do?"

Memories from the one summer her brother worked at the bakery surfaced. "More like what didn't he do? When my parents refused to let him get a job somewhere else, he set out to make sure our mother didn't want him at the bakery. At first it was just little things. Showing up late, taking extra long breaks. When that didn't work he stepped up his efforts. The final straw was when he started a small fire in the kitchen. He still insists that it was an accident, but no one believes him."

Across the table Trent cringed. "I can see how that would get him banned. Is he your only brother?"

Addie opened her mouth to answer, when Chloe called out to her from the front counter. "Your coffee is ready, Addie." Addie didn't even manage to push her chair back before Trent stood.

"I'll get it for you."

A girl could get used to this. From the table she followed Trent's movements as he crossed to the front counter and she almost sighed out loud. Watching the guy walk was just so… she didn't even know how to describe it. Yet, she knew no one should look that good while simply crossing a room.

At the counter he said something to Chloe, who still stood there, and in return she smiled at him. Then with her coffee in hand, he started back toward their table. The minute he turned his back on her cousin, Chloe flashed her a thumps up sign, then used her hand to signal Addie to call her later.

With the same athletic grace he used when he walked, Trent retook his seat, his attention once again focused on her. "So is he your only brother?" He asked, picking up their conversation right where they left off.

Addie cocked her head to the side and wondered if he asked all his business associates such questions. "If only," she answered after deciding it didn't matter how he treated his other associates. "I have four, all older than me." Even she heard the hint of exasperation that crept into her voice. She adored her brothers, really she did, but having four older brothers was sometimes like having four additional fathers.

At her comment Trent laughed, a deep rich sound that soon had her smiling despite her best efforts to maintain a straight face.

"You sound like my sister. The two of you make it sound like having brothers is worse than death. I'll have to introduce you to her, I think you'd get along well."

Addie doubted that. She'd get along about as well with

Allison Sherbrooke as she would with the Queen of England. In fact, she probably had as much in common with the Queen as she did Trent's sister. "You try being not just the only girl in the family, but the youngest, too. Then get back to me."

Trent raised his cup in a gesture of surrender, but amusement remained in his eyes. "Fair enough."

With no idea where to take their conversation next, she looked down at her untouched snack and broke it in half. When nothing else came to mind she settled on talk of the projects he'd hired her for but had not yet asked about. "I've started on some preliminary designs for your house. I hope to have something rough for you by the end of next week. Depending on what you like or dislike, I can make changes."

"I'm looking forward to seeing what you come up with." On the table Trent laced his fingers together, the movement causing his shirt sleeve to inch up just enough to uncover a large expensive-looking watch on his wrist, another stark reminder of just who sat across from her. "I read that the city has WaterFire scheduled for this Saturday night. I've never been. Have you?"

Addie shook her head. "Almost made it once last summer, but then it rained and I decided not to go."

"If you not busy, would you care to join me? We could have dinner first."

A multitude of questions, ones she should never voice, popped up in her head all clamoring for answers, answers she couldn't even begin to speculate on. "That sounds like fun." *Great choice of words.*

Regardless of her exact choice of words, Trent smiled, pleased with her response. "Excellent. I'll pick you up at six o'clock then?"

"I'll be ready."

TRENT REMOVED his suit pants and pulled on a pair of jeans. On his way out of his room he tossed the pants into his laundry basket with the rest of the dry cleaning. After grabbing a cold can of soda from the refrigerator, he retreated to his entertainment room for a night of mindless television. Long spans of solitude were not his thing. In fact, he'd spent more nights alone since his recent return to Providence than he had in the last five years combined. Yet if the small sacrifice now earned him a seat in the Senate, he'd manage. If only Jake or one of his brothers was around. Their presence would help the situation.

Not too much longer. This afternoon he'd taken one step closer to winning Addison over. Next week at this time their relationship status would be on the front of every society page and magazine cover. He had no doubt about that. And while Addie had questions regarding his intentions—he'd seen them in her expression that afternoon—she hadn't hesitated to accept his invitation for that weekend. A weekend he was looking forward to with anticipation and not only because isolation didn't suit him.

Unlike the numerous women he'd spent time with over the years, and there had been plenty, Addie made him laugh. She teased him and shared information about herself without first worrying about how he might interpret her words. She let her true feelings regarding family show rather than try to distance herself from them as many people he met did. At the same time she never kissed up to him. At least as far as he could tell, she treated him the same way she would any other person or client.

Taking a gulp from the soda can in his hand, he propped his feet up on the coffee table as he planned their upcoming night out. First, they would have a romantic dinner at perhaps Lucerne. One of their secluded tables would do. Then they'd take a stroll down to Waterplace Park to watch WaterFire. Afterward, he'd take her back here for a drink or two. Once back at his place, he'd let her determine just how far things went. While

Marty complained things with Addie were moving too slow, Trent disagreed. If he moved too fast it might spook her. While she was a well-educated businesswoman, she came across as a woman who didn't date a lot. Hell, she even blushed from time to time. Truthfully, it wouldn't shock him if he learned she hadn't gone on a single date since the end of her last relationship. And thanks to Marty's research he knew that relationship ended more than a year ago. Although if that was true, the men she came into contact with must be blind.

Addie didn't resemble the supermodels that walked the runways in Paris or New York or the actresses that he'd dated over the years. Rather, she reminded him more of *Sports Illustrated*'s recent mega star that had graced their summer swimsuit issue. She had curves in all the right places and didn't look as if she'd fall over if a strong breeze came through.

A picture of Addie dressed in a bikini like the one worn on the cover of this year's swimsuit issue formed in his mind, and Trent smiled at the mental image. While he found fashion models and movie stars just as attractive as the next guy, he'd always favored those who looked fit and healthy. Those that looked like they ate more than once a month. His expert eye told him that description fit Addie and he was looking forward to finding that out for himself.

Trent took another swig from his soda, and he considered whether or not to return Marty's call tonight. He'd left a message earlier in the afternoon inquiring about a status update. Should he call him now and let him know that things were progressing as planned or wait until later that weekend? *Let him wait.* Marty worked for him, not the other way around. If he chose to take things slow with Addie that was his business.

Pulling his phone from his pocket, Trent switched the device off. Then he turned on the television and settled in for another night alone.

EIGHT

Halfway out the door Saturday night, Trent turned and went back into the kitchen. An hour earlier the florist had delivered a dozen long stem roses to his apartment per his instructions. Roses he intended for Addie. It'd be rather difficult to give her the flowers when he picked her up if they remained on his kitchen counter. Rarely did he bring flowers to a woman. In fact, the last time he'd given flowers to anyone it had been as part of his sister's birthday present. Allison, much like their mother, adored flowers. Addie struck him as the type who'd appreciate flowers, and a lot was riding on their date tonight. Despite their earlier interactions, tonight he needed to make it clear his interest ran deeper than simple business. At the same time, he needed to come across as sincere and the type of man she would want in her life. The playboy in the media needed to disappear.

Confident he had all he needed, Trent closed the door and headed for his private elevator. *Yup, tonight's perhaps the most important date of your life. Don't fuck it up.* The elevator door closed on that thought and began its way down to the lobby.

When he pulled into Addie's driveway a short while later, only her Corolla sat parked in front of her condo. Her windows remained open and when he approached the front door he heard the sound of country music. During their few meetings they'd never discussed music preferences, but he'd pegged her as someone who listened to the latest pop music much like his sister. Country music hadn't even crossed his mind.

After knocking on the door, Trent waited and took in the neighborhood around him. All the homes on both sides of the street looked identical. Originally built at the turn of the twentieth century for the factory workers and their families, the narrow two-floor homes had at some point in the past decade or so been updated and sold as individual condos. Much like her neighbors on either side of her, she'd added some personal touches to make her home somewhat different from the rest. She'd painted her front door a vibrant red and hung a wreath on it. She'd also added solar lights on either side of her short walkway and hung a wind chime from the overhang above the door.

His eyes had just finished their sweep of the houses nearby when he spotted the sedan driving down the street. While much like the other cars in the neighborhood, Trent got the sense that this one didn't belong here. True, its slow speed could be due to the driver who wasn't familiar with the area looking for a specific house number, but something told him the driver had other reasons for being around. As Trent continued to watch, the car pulled to the curb three units down and the driver remained inside.

"Hi, Trent," Addie said appearing at the door. "Come on in." She pushed the screen door open for him.

He glanced over at the sedan one last time, then turned his full attention to Addie. This evening she had on a white sundress that reminded him a great deal of the one Marilyn Monroe wore in the iconic picture of her from *The Seven Year Itch*. The snow-white color emphasized her sun-bronzed skin. She'd pulled all her hair up, leaving her neck exposed, and damn if he didn't want to touch her to see if her skin was in fact as smooth as it looked. Stepping forward, he entered the house and placed a kiss on her cheek. "These are for you." He held out the bouquet of roses.

Her eyes widened, but she didn't make a move to take them. Then she smiled and accepted the bundle, bringing the flowers toward her face.

"They're beautiful." She inhaled the scent of them, her eyes drifting closed. "Give me a minute to put them in water and then we can go." She looked back up at him, her expression telling him so much. She wasn't accustomed to receiving gifts from men, flowers or otherwise.

"Okay. We're in no rush."

"I'm all set except for this," she answered, turning and leading him down the narrow hallway to the kitchen.

Like her arms and face, the skin on her back looked smooth and sun kissed. No tan lines marred the bare flawless skin, and he wondered if she lay out in her backyard topless. With no effort on his part, an image of her in her tiny fenced backyard sprang up. In his vision she relaxed on a padded chaise lounge, her hair tied up much like it was now wearing the bottoms to a string bikini and nothing else. A pair of sunglasses protected her eyes while country music played in the background.

"I've never seen roses this color." Addie pulled a glass vase from a cupboard near the stove. "They're really gorgeous, but you didn't have to bring me flowers."

Trent's fantasy image evaporated. "I wanted to." He watched as she trimmed the pink champagne-colored roses. "I made us a reservation at Lucerne. Have you ever been?"

Addie shook her head, the tendrils she'd left free swaying as she arranged the roses in the vase. "No, but I've heard about them. The Phantom Gourmet ranked them as one of the best restaurants in New England last year." She stuck the final rose in the vase and then admired her work. "All set."

"After dinner I thought we'd head over to Waterplace Park for WaterFire. According to the schedule they have an old-fashioned big band performing tonight. It's not my kind of music, but it should still be a nice night." Trent followed her back to the front door, pausing only when she stopped to turn of the music. "If you'd rather do something else, just say the word."

Joining him at the door, she headed outside. "No, I've been looking forward to WaterFire tonight."

He reached for Addie's hand as they walked over to his car. He'd done the same thing the afternoon they'd walked though his home in Newport. That day much like now, he'd done it as if on autopilot. The action hadn't been thought out or planned to elicit a particular response. Rather he'd done it because he enjoyed the physical contact. He liked the way her smaller hand fit inside his, as if they'd been meant for each other. He enjoyed the feel of her soft skin without any flashy jewelry digging into his own flesh. In fact, Addie wore little jewelry at all. Tonight she wore a silver necklace, tiny silver earrings, and a matching silver bracelet. The amount of jewelry she had on tonight was the most he'd ever seen on her. During their previous meetings she'd worn nothing more than a watch. Whether that was because she disliked jewelry or simply didn't own much he wasn't sure, but he'd find out. If it turned out she liked it but couldn't afford it, he'd rectify that situation.

Stopping next to his car, he pulled open the door. "Is something wrong?" he asked when she didn't move.

"I've been seeing that car a lot. Or at least I think it's the same car."

Trent followed her line of sight and spotted the same dark-colored sedan that had caught his attention earlier. From her driveway, it appeared empty.

"I thought I saw movement inside, but now it looks empty," Addie said, a hint of unease in her voice.

"We'll get the license plate on the way by and I'll have

someone look into it." Already he had an idea of what the car's owner was up to. He'd bet his new Bugatti Veyron that the car belonged to a photographer out hoping to get a juicy picture or two.

"You can do that?" Addie asked as she settled herself in the passenger seat.

Trent nodded. "Trust me. We'll figure out who it is. Don't worry about it." Closing the door, he glanced once more time toward the sedan just in time to see a figure move inside, a camera with a long lens blocking his face. Yup, a photographer. Not a huge surprise. Since the first photo of him and Addie appeared in the paper, he'd expected to see more, but as of yet none had appeared. Obviously that was about to change. Marty would be pleased, as it would fall in line with his plan.

At the curb in front of Lucerne, his favorite Italian restaurant in Providence, a uniformed valet accepted Trent's keys before he walked around to the curb where Addie waited for him. On the short ride from her house into the city, she'd filled him in on the designs for his home, making the ride feel a bit more like a business meeting than a date. He let her go on without interrupting; hoping that by the time they reached the restaurant she'd be more relaxed. Though she didn't say as much, her stiff posture and clenched hands gave away her anxiety.

"Fred confirmed that he completed the painting of your office. Are you satisfied with the color?" Addie sat in the chair he pulled out for her.

Placing his hands on her bare shoulders, he leaned down toward her ear. "It's perfect, but that's the last I want to hear about work tonight. Anything relating to my office or house can wait until Monday."

Addie turned her head and tilted her face toward his, her lips only inches away from his. Tonight she wore a light pink lipstick and his first instinct was to cover her mouth with his and kiss away every last inch of color.

"Okay. What do you want to talk about then?" Her lips moved before he could kiss her.

"You." He moved to his own seat before he gave into the temptation to kiss her. While he had every intention of doing that tonight, this wasn't the time or place.

"Me?" she asked with amusement. "I think it would a more interesting conversation if we talked about you." She accepted the menu the waiter held out to her, and Trent held back his response until the man left the table.

Putting down his menu, he folded his hands on the table. "Ask me anything you want."

"You might regret saying that." Her lips curved into a mischievous smile. "But to start what do you recommend for dinner?" Addie opened the large menu still in her hand.

ORDERS TAKEN, the waiter disappeared once again leaving her alone with Trent. Although several other tables in the exclusive restaurant were occupied, they sat tucked away from prying eyes and ears. Once again the notion that she, Addison Raimono, was on a date with legendary playboy Trent Sherbrooke had her questioning her sanity, something she'd been doing since he asked her to dinner. At first she'd tried to convince herself this was just another business dinner, similar to the one in Newport at the Spiced Pear. But any hopes of doing that evaporated when she opened the door and saw him holding roses. No one, not even Trent Sherbrooke, showed up for a business meal with roses in hand.

"So you said I could ask you anything, right?" A hundred various questions filled her mind, some she'd never have the audacity to ask.

"Ask away. I don't want there to be any secrets between us."

A sliver of excitement pierced her stomach at his response. "What kind of music do you like?" Okay, it wasn't the most personal question she had, but it was a safe, unobtrusive place to start.

Immediately, Trent laughed as he reached for his wine. "Of all the things you could ask, you want to know what kind of music I like?"

At the sound of his laughter, her body relaxed. Her shoulders dipped and the tiny ball of nerves in her stomach disappeared. Somehow his laugh, deep and contagious, touched her body's physical responses. It had done the same thing during their previous meetings.

"I thought I'd start out with the simple questions and work my way up."

"A woman with a plan. I like it." The sensuous undertones in his voice sent another arrow of excitement through her body. "I listen mostly to hard rock like they play on HJY," he answered referring to a popular rock station out of Providence. "Sometimes I will listen to classic bands like Pink Floyd or Zeppelin."

Addie didn't need a mirror to know she'd cringed at his response.

"I take it you like something else?" Trent asked confirming her suspicion.

"I'd rather listen to country myself. Right now Miranda Lambert and Lady Antebellum are two of my favorites." This time Trent cringed and shook his head. "I do like the Rolling Stones and Aerosmith," she said. While not her favorite, she'd grown up listening to the two bands, thanks to her parents, and she'd come to like much of their stuff.

Across from her, Trent took a sip from his wine. "I'll never complain if the Stones or Aerosmith are on."

Addie and Trent continued sharing tidbits of information with each other as they waited for their meals and through dinner. Each little nugget Trent shared pushed his persona as a spoiled rich playboy further and further to the back of her mind and the new image she had of him continued to grow. This new image showcased a man who, despite media reports, wasn't superficial and full of himself. Rather, he was charming and polite while at the same time funny and, for the most part, down to earth. He never acted, at least not with her, as if he considered himself better than everyone else and he didn't seem to take himself too seriously.

"Okay, my turn to ask some questions," Trent said as they walked from the parking garage toward Waterplace Park. So far she'd asked all the questions. "And I promise to start with the easy ones." He slipped his arm across her shoulders and pulled her against his side sending her heart rate dangerously high.

"Fair enough." Not sure if it was the right move or not, Addie slid an arm around his waist as they strolled toward their destination.

They crossed the street and then Trent said, "I know your mom and dad and your cousins live around here. What about your brothers? Other than the story about the one who started the kitchen fire, you don't talk too much about them."

"Tom's the closest. He's stationed at Fort Devens in Massachusetts. Frank is at Camp Pendleton in California and Rock is stationed in Quantico, Virginia. Now that Jon is in the reserves, he lives up in Maine."

"I'm guessing Rock is a nickname."

"Yeah. He's real name is Rocco, but he hates it. My parents gave all my brothers traditional Italian names."

"Frank is a traditional Italian name?"

All her brother's hated their legal given names and would be furious if they knew she was sharing them. "Another nickname. His given name is Franco. All my brothers use nicknames. Tom is short for Tommaso and Jon is short for Giovanni. If you ever want to get on their bad sides just use their given names."

Trent laughed at her comment. "I'll remember that. So they're all in the military?"

The sound of music and voices reached Addie before she

saw the musicians tuning up for their evening performance, a crowd already gathered nearby. "All Marines, like my dad and grandfather, except Tom. He likes to be different so he joined the Army after college."

Trent navigated them toward a less congested area near the railing that overlooked the basin where bonfires would soon be lit. "Your dad's a Marine, too?"

Moving to stand behind her as more people crowded in around them, he pulled her against him and looped his arms around her waist. The warmth from his body seeped through his clothes and into her skin, setting her body on fire. It had been a long time since a man had held her, yet it had never felt like this before. "Technically, once a Marine, always a Marine," she said when she remembered that he'd asked her a question. "He retired a while ago and has worked as a prison guard for years now. Everyone on my dad's side of the family has been in the military except my cousin David, who's only sixteen, and me. It's almost an unspoken expectation."

"So you moved around a lot growing up?" He rested his chin on the top of her head driving home their intimate position.

She ran her tongue over her lips and swallowed before she answered. "Not too much. Nothing like my two oldest brothers Jon and Tom. My dad retired when I was seven and we moved to Rhode Island. All my mom's family was around here and my dad's sister was stationed at the Navy base here at the time."

A gong echoed around them signaling that the sun had set. On cue, fires came alive thanks to fire tenders in boats traveling the river, and the musicians started. Overhead a scattering of stars peeked out from the clouds, which had rolled in while they ate dinner.

"My dad was disappointed when I didn't follow the tradition. We had more than one heated conversation about how it was everyone's duty to serve their country." Even now their arguments about her decision to pursue a different career path remained fresh in her mind.

"And what about your mom?" He asked a perfectly logical question, yet she couldn't hold back the groan it produced. "I take it she wanted you to follow that path as well?"

Addie shook her head as a different set of arguments flowed back. "She was okay with that decision, but she wanted me to study business and take over management of the bakeries. The idea of doing that bored me to death. And when I told them my plan to study interior design they both flipped. Even now my mom tells me it's not too late to get my MBA and take over for my grandfather when he steps down in a few years."

"It's hard when your family wants one thing and you want something else. My cousin used to butt heads with my uncle all the time. Thankfully, my career goals have always corresponded more or less with my father's expectations." Trent's comment provided more insight into his personal life, something he seemed to have no trouble doing. "So your family is the reason you moved back to Rhode Island and opened shop here?" he asked.

The scent of burning wood drifted around her as she watched the flickering flames dance on the water's surface. The sight was beautiful and almost hypnotizing. "More or less. There is also less competition here in Providence than in Boston." On the river a torch-lit boat glided past and her eyes followed its path away from them. "What about you? What brought you here?" Everyone knew Trent and his siblings had been born in Rhode Island and spent at least part of their lives there. But he was a man who could live anywhere in the world and she knew he'd only just recently returned to the state.

"Hey, I thought it was my turn to ask the questions?" Trent asked, pretending to sound outraged.

Addie squeezed his hand. "I'll owe you one."

Trent's arms dropped from around her waist and he took a

step back. Immediately, she missed the solid feel of his body next to hers. "Okay, but let's walk a little as we talk. I read it's the only proper way to experience WaterFire." Like he'd done in Newport, he entwined their fingers together and joined the crowd strolling along the river's path. "Rhode Island has always been my legal state of residence even though for the past few years I haven't spent much time here." As he spoke his thumb rubbed the palm of her hand causing her already heightened senses to escalate a bit closer to the stars.

"I've always known I'd run for a public office someday. Last spring I decided it was time so I left my previous position at Sherbrooke Enterprises and moved back here with the intention of running for Senate."

"Why Senate and not the House?" Since her American government class freshman year of high school, politics had interested her and she'd often wondered what influenced a person to run for one particular office as opposed to another, especially when it came to the House of Representative and the Senate. While both were distinct bodies with different roles, they seemed similar to her in numerous ways.

"My Uncle Warren was a Senator, as was my grandfather. And the party needs to hold onto Senator Harrison's seat to maintain the majority in the Senate," Trent answered, referring to a well-respected Senator who had served in the United States Senate for thirty years. Most had expected him to serve until the day he died, but he had recently announced that he would not seek reelection when his term ended, despite his popularity.

"Do you think you'll ever run for President like your uncle?"

"Now you're going to owe me two questions." He gave her side a playful pinch. "Between you and me, yes, I'd like to, but at this point I'm not ready to commit publicly."

His answer made perfect sense considering who he was and who he was related to. Still, the notion she was out with someone who might one day be one of the most powerful men in the world felt surreal. She had enough worries and issues to handle on her own plate. She couldn't comprehend the type of issues the President must deal with on a daily basis. More importantly, she wouldn't want to deal with all the President had to face and until now she'd never met anyone who would even consider taking on such an endeavor.

"Now that you've managed to sneak in two extra questions, it's my turn again." Trent navigated them around a group of people that had stopped in the middle of the path, never once releasing her hand. "Do you ever regret leaving Ducat and Wakefield and going out on your own?"

Addie watched a boat as it made its way down the river, the fire tender on board ensuring that the giant bonfires remained aflame. In the two years since she'd opened Designs by Addison no one had ever asked her that question. When her family, specifically her mom, brought up the matter of her career choices it was just to remind her she could always close up shop and take a more active role at the bakeries. That wasn't to say she hadn't considered whether or not her decision to branch out on her own had been wise or not.

"Yes and no," she said admitting for the first time to anyone her true feelings. "I love being in complete control, but I do miss the security of working for Ducat and Wakefield. Running a business, even one as small as mine, entails more than I anticipated." She hoped the desperation and anxiety she sometimes suffered from regarding her business didn't seep into her voice.

"If there's ever anything I can help with, just ask."

She heard nothing but complete sincerity in his voice. Even still, she doubted she could ever ask him for help of any kind. Not only was he a virtual stranger, but someone who helped run a multi-billion dollar company didn't have the time to help a small fledging company such as hers.

"Thank you, but you've already helped me. When people learn that I've designed for a Sherbrooke it will boost my reputation," she answered, anxious to move the topic of their conversation away from her business. "You still have one more question you can ask me."

"Are you busy tomorrow afternoon?"

For a moment she wondered whom she might be able to ask to cover her shift at the bakery, but just as quickly she killed the idea. While her business had started picking up since the picture in the paper, who knew how long it would last? If she hoped to keep herself afloat, she needed the extra money from her part-time job. "I'm scheduled for a shift at the bakery from seven until two and afterwards I need to catch up on some paperwork." She hated admitting to him she still worked at the bakery, but at the same time it did no good to lie.

He glanced over at her, the flames from the torches on the bridge casting his face in shadows, making it difficult to see his expression and gauge his reaction to her answer. She suspected few women ever told him they had other obligations when he asked them out.

"Does that mean you want to call it an early night? I thought we could go back to my apartment for a little bit before I take you home, but we can do that some other time if you want."

In the past two years or so she hadn't done much dating, but she still recognized the signs that a guy was interested in her. And although difficult to accept, Trent was sending out a lot of signals in that direction. "No, not that early. I've worked enough at the bakery that if need be I could do it half asleep and with one arm tied behind my back." At this point in her life she wouldn't have sought out a relationship, she just didn't have the time. Yet she enjoyed Trent's company and saw no real down side to spending time with him.

Trent squeezed her hand as they continued walking. "Good. How about we head to my apartment now? You can see the fires along the river from there, too."

Already by agreeing to dinner with him she'd crossed that

professional line and entered into dangerous territory. And while the businesswoman in her suggested she consider carefully before stepping any further over the line, the woman in her urged her to close her eyes and leap toward him, see what happened now and worry about the possible repercussions later. In the end, she gagged the businesswoman in her and stuffed her in the closet. "I'd love to."

His lips, the very ones she dreamed about kissing, formed a smile and for a brief moment the world around them disappeared. Then just as quickly as the moment came, the music from the band registered again as did the other people around them.

"Great. I promise not to get you home too late."

It was a short ride to Trent's apartment, and soon Addie found herself stepping off his private elevator.

"After you." Trent pushed open the door to his apartment.

Addie took a step forward but stopped just inside and looked back at him. "Do you want me to take my shoes off?"

Trent followed her in and let the door close behind them. "Whatever would make you feel at home."

Addie moistened her lips and considered his words. Again, his words made it sound as if he intended something to develop between them, at least that was how she interpreted them. Turning forward again, she moved further into the apartment's entrance, and across the glossy hardwood floor.

She'd driven by The Hillcrest more times than she could count since its construction five years ago. Not once during all the time had she considered or cared who lived there. After all, The Hillcrest was the city's premier apartment building. No one she knew could afford the price they asked for even the one-bedroom apartments. Given the building's luxury status, it made perfect sense that Trent lived not only in the building but also in its penthouse, which occupied the entire top two floors.

Without taking another step forward she took in her

surroundings and hoped Trent hadn't heard her jaw hit the floor. Since the beginning of her career she'd been in and worked on several luxury projects, but this place put all except one to shame. It quite literally was a designer's dream come to life. Not one detail had been overlooked, and judging by the looks of it, no expense had been spared.

"Why don't you check out the view while I pour us some wine?" Warm hands came down on her shoulders and caressed her skin as they made their way down her arms. "Do you prefer white or red?"

Even with space between them she felt the heat coming from his body and she began to lean back toward him seeking the intimate embrace they'd shared earlier that night.

"Or if you'd rather I can make you something else, perhaps a Cosmo?"

Her bare back rubbed against the front of his shirt, the friction causing goose bumps to form on her arms and her answer to Trent's question slipped from her mind. Closing her eyes, she focused on the rise and fall of his chest against her as he breathed. Would he consider her crazy if she turned right now and kissed him? And even if he did, it might be worth it.

"Are you cold?" He moved so that they stood face-to-face. His hand moved back up her arms, but instead of getting rid of the goose bumps, which must have been his purpose, she shivered under his hands.

"I just got a little chill. I'm fine." She glanced away as she spoke. When he opened his mouth as if to argue she beat him to it. "Really, I'm fine. See, the chill is already gone." Addie held her arm out toward him, the goose bumps now gone.

Without looking away from her face, he lifted her hand toward his mouth and kissed her just above the knuckles. "If you say so, but if that changes let me know."

Voice gone, thanks to his brief sign of affection, she nodded and let herself get lost in the moment.

"I want you to be comfortable here." His voice became husky and he took a step closer so that now they touched from chest to thigh. "Because I hope to see you here a lot in the future." The words left his mouth and before her brain could finish processing them, he lowered his head toward hers.

Adrenaline shot through her as her mind registered his intent, and Addie's eyes fluttered closed just as his lips made contact with hers. At first his lips moved gently against hers, a mere wisp of a kiss. Prepared to lose herself in the moment, Addie slid her arms over Trent's shoulders and clasped her hands together, grateful for the extra inch or two her heels gave her. As if encouraged by her response, Trent deepened the kiss and used his tongue to tease her lips apart until she opened for him.

FINALLY. Since he'd picked her up he'd wanted to taste her. Back in her kitchen he'd contemplated kissing her, but had held back determined not to rush anything. Only by using all his self-restraint had he managed to hold back then.

Changing the angle of his head, he rubbed his tongue against hers and an intense urge to walk her up to his bedroom, remove her dress, and just look at her filled his head. Granted he'd desired plenty of women before, yet somehow this time it was different, more intense and overwhelming. And while his body urged him to just do it, his rational self said otherwise. Before tonight he'd never clearly suggested he wanted anything other than a professional relationship with her. If he pushed things too fast it might scare her. And while he'd been known to sleep with a woman he'd known for less time than he'd known Addie, he pegged her for the type who didn't have sex on a first date.

Rein it in. There's no need to rush things. After one more pass over her lips, Trent dug into his self-restraint and pulled his mouth away from Addie. At first she remained still, her eyes closed, her lips moist and rosy from their kiss. In the seconds before she opened her eyes, his body told him to once again take possession of her mouth to kiss her until she wanted him as much as his body wanted her. Reminding himself she was different than the usual women he dated, Trent took a step back and hoped space would get the message from his brain to his body.

As if waking from sleep, Addie's eyes fluttered open and met his gaze. He knew the moment she processed their kiss. A hint of color, almost impossible to see unless you'd been watching, crept into her face and she glanced away before meeting his eyes again.

"If I'm going to be spending time here, maybe you should give me a tour."

Her words sent a ripple of unexpected happiness through him that had nothing to do with Marty's plan. Rather his happiness had everything to do with his desire to spend time with Addie and get to know her better. Something he'd want even if Marty didn't believe she was the key to salvaging his reputation.

Trent reached out and brushed his fingers across her cheek. "How about I pour us some wine first and then I'll show you around. If you want to check out the view before they extinguish the fires, go ahead. I'll be right back."

"I forgot about that," she said and took a step away from him.

He watched her walk away toward the living room that over-looked the river and allowed himself a moment to appreciate the tanned skin on her back and legs. Then, before he changed his mind about taking things slow with her, he crossed into his kitchen to the built-in wine refrigerator.

"You were right. The view from up here is great. The height gives you a whole different perspective," Addie said, her voice reaching him in the kitchen.

"You'll find I'm right every once in awhile. I try not to let it happen too often though," Trent said as he picked up the two wine glasses. "If you're right too much, people start to expect it all the time from you."

Addie turned her back to the window and faced him as he approached, an amused smile lighting up her face. "A guy who admits he's usually wrong—I like it."

Trent stopped dead in his tracks. "Wait a minute, I never said I'm usually wrong."

Walking up to him, she took a glass from his hand. "Sounded that way to me."

Leaning in toward her, he covered her lips with his for a brief kiss that he ended before his desire overtook his common sense. "I guess I'll just have to show you then." He took a sip from his glass, giving his mouth something to do besides kiss her.

"You can try," she said with humor in her voice. "In the meantime, how about that tour?"

Trent took one more sip from his wine and then set his glass on an end table. "Let's start down here, then head upstairs." Taking her hand, he led her toward the back of the apartment and his home office.

After a quick tour through the apartment, Trent led her back into the living room where they spent two hours talking about everything from movies to music. Although he would have loved to do so much more than that, he decided not to rush things with Addie. So although it left his body aching to touch her, he took her home around eleven o'clock.

NINE

Late Friday afternoon Addie examined the kitchen floor plan she'd designed for the Meads and their pre-Civil War era Bristol home one last time before meeting with them that evening. It had taken a few attempts, but Addie believed she now had a plan that fit their vision and also their budget, a task that was sometimes the most difficult part of her job.

Once satisfied that the plan required no further changes, she closed the open file on her computer and brought up her plans for Trent's house. Despite her arguments, he'd insisted that she put her other projects first and only work on his when she had the time. According to him, he had no set time frame for getting the house done, so she didn't need to rush. Even with his insistence she made sure she got in some work on the project—which was still her biggest one—every day, but she'd stopped informing him of that fact during his nightly phone calls.

The calls had started the previous Sunday following their date on Saturday night. She'd been home a few hours from the bakery and had made it through half of her paperwork when her cell phone rang. Although not one for long phone conversations, they'd talked for about an hour, and before they'd ended he'd promised to call the following night after his meeting with his campaign advisor. Like clockwork his call came again Monday and Tuesday night around seven o'clock. At the end of their conversation on Tuesday, he'd asked her to meet him for dinner on Wednesday. Her shift at the bakery forced her to decline, but she'd suggested Thursday instead, which he had to decline because of a late afternoon meeting in Maine. With their schedules not cooperating, they'd agreed to get together Saturday afternoon and she wanted to show him the progress she'd made on his house plans. Thanks to the size of the home, the unlimited budget she had to work with, and the open time frame, the sky was truly the limit for the project, and it had taken Addie some time before she settled on a style she believed Trent would like and one that would also preserve the look and feel of the home. Now that she'd settled on the style though, her creative side had taken over and she had at least the plans for the kitchen almost complete. The plan now on her computer screen was perhaps the best work she'd ever done, and the idea of showing Trent excited her almost as much as the thought of spending time with him again.

Using her mouse, she changed the size of one of the kitchen islands she put into her plans as her mind wandered back to their phone conversations over the past week. During each of them he'd been charming and funny while at the same time open and honest. He answered any questions she asked and encouraged her to ask him anything at all. At the same time though, he kept his questions a little more general and allowed her to decide just how much she wanted to reveal. And while on Sunday she'd kept some of her answers less personal, that had changed as the week went on. In fact, the night before they'd gotten on the topic of their best friends as children and she'd admitted to him how angry and hurt she'd been when her best friend of two years told her she no longer wanted to be friends and that she'd only been friends with her to get close to her older brother Rock, something she'd never told anyone, not even her cousin Chloe who was like a sister. In return, Trent had told her some crazy stories about things he'd done with his best friend and cousin, Jake.

Addie changed to another page, which showed the kitchen from a different angle, and adjusted the paint color on the walls. While she preferred the first color she'd used, the lighter version brightened the room more. The home's original designer hadn't considered that the homeowners would ever want to use and enjoy the kitchen space. Rather, it had been designed for hired help. In order to brighten the room and give it a better view of the ocean, she'd already added two additional windows. The lighter paint shade should be the finishing touch.

Hitting okay on the keyboard, she watched the change take effect on the screen. The new lighter shade of green brightened the room but didn't look quite right. Addie reached for the keyboard prepared to darken the color by a degree but paused at the knock on her office door.

"Can I come in?"

At the sound of Trent's voice, Addie spun her chair around and found Trent standing in her doorway.

"Of course." Addie smiled, her eyes drawn to the outline of his broad shoulders, which filled out the suit jacket he wore. "I thought you were going to be in Connecticut until tonight."

Trent placed two iced coffees on the desk and then slipped off his jacket, hanging it over the back of a chair. "I finished up early and couldn't wait until tomorrow to see you."

His words caused unexpected warmth to surge through her. Before she could answer, he came around the desk and kissed her. In response, her heart pounded an erratic rhythm as his lips moved against hers and she hoped her heart didn't suffer any permanent damage.

"I wasn't sure I'd make it back before you left the office," Trent said after he pulled away ending their kiss. "It seemed worth a shot, so I raced back when my meeting ended." He dropped into the seat on the other side of her desk and rolled up his shirtsleeves.

Addie reached for the iced coffee he'd brought her in an effort to keep herself from sighing like a lovesick thirteen-year-old at his thoughtful admission. "I don't have a lot of time. The Meads are due at six thirty, but I'm glad you're here."

Trent picked up his own drink and raised it toward his mouth, her eyes following his every move. "Is that your design for them?" He pointed at the computer screen with his cup.

After a mental shake that refocused her thoughts, she looked at the screen. "No, this is my design for your kitchen. I wanted to have it ready to show you tomorrow. I also started the designs for the two master bathrooms. What do you think?" Beneath her desk, her foot twitched as she waited for his answer. She'd spent hours on the design. What if he decided it wasn't good enough? No one wanted to hear that, especially after all the effort she'd put into it.

Trent stood and walked around to her side of the desk. "It's fabulous," he said from behind her as he examined the picture on the screen. "I hadn't considered adding extra windows to the room, but those above the sink look as if they belong there. And I love the idea of the two islands." He pointed to one of the islands in the picture. "If we put some stools at this one we can eat and enjoy the view from these windows."

A new unexpected warmth spread through her when he insinuated they'd be spending time together in the kitchen. "What about the color of the cabinets. Are they too dark?" She heard the little wobble in her voice and hoped Trent hadn't noticed.

Warm flesh came in contact with her arms as Trent's hand settled on her upper arm. "No. They're just right for the room. And the subtle carvings over here give the room just the right amount of elegance without going overboard." With his free hand he pointed to the carvings on one of the islands. "I approve of the whole design." Trent's hand moved away from her arm and he spun her chair around so that she faced him. "I can't wait to see what else you've come up with." Taking her by the hand, he pulled her to her feet. "But remember what I said. I'm in no rush on this project. Work on it when you have the time." Before she could protest he leaned in toward her. "The house isn't going anywhere and neither am I." His lips brushed against her as he spoke the last part of his sentence.

Addie leaned into him as Trent took full possession of her lips, caressing her mouth more than kissing it. As the kiss continued, she felt his heart thudding against hers and a different jolt of excitement shot through her. While she'd never considered herself ugly, she'd never thought of herself as the type who could arouse a legendary playboy like Trent. Yet, judging by his kiss and his body's reaction, he desired her just as much as she did him. When the need for air outweighed the utter enjoyment she experienced with Trent's mouth on hers, Addie pulled back.

"What time will you be done tonight?" Trent asked, his deep blue eyes fixed on her.

Unable to look away, she shrugged. "I'm not sure. If they like my proposal maybe a little after seven, but if they want a lot of changes it could be later."

"Will you come by my place when you're done?" he asked, his voice low and seductive. "I don't want to wait until tomorrow to see you again."

"Are you sure? It might be late." Although he looked as handsome as ever, Trent appeared tired and, thanks to their phone conversations that week, she knew he'd spent a lot of time traveling around New England for meetings.

"Positive." He placed a kiss on her forehead. "It's almost six thirty so I'm going to head out now. Just come over when you're done." His lips brushed against hers again. "Have a good meeting and I'll see you in a little while."

When the door closed behind him, Addie dropped back into her office chair, a giddy smile on her face. Trent had truly missed her. During their conversations he'd said as much, but she'd chalked it up as something he said to everyone. She could no longer do that. He'd rushed back to see her and invited her over despite their original plans to wait until tomorrow. And while she loved talking to him during the week, she'd reminded herself over and over that Trent wasn't known for his long-term relationships, so she should be prepared for a fun but short-lived fling. Each time she reminded herself of that, she'd think of their time together so far and how his actions didn't fit with his persona. Was it possible that he viewed this thing between them as different from his past relationships? *Either way is fine.* Addie repeated the same line she'd told herself all week. If her and Trent's involvement ended up being short-lived, that was okay because she didn't have time for a relationship right now anyway. On the other hand, if things lasted she'd be happy, too. She enjoyed her time with him, and if she was honest about it, he made her feel more alive than she had in a long time.

Reaching for the iced coffee he brought, she took a sip. Yup, whatever happened, happened. She'd be fine whatever path this thing with Trent took. *Liar,* a tiny voice in the back of her head whispered. *You want this relationship to last.* Addie took another sip from her drink and blocked out the voice calling her bluff, then turned back toward her computer and waited for the Meads.

Addie's appointment with the Meads went so smoothly, she almost pinched herself just to make sure she wasn't dreaming. The couple arrived right on time, both coming directly from work. Both loved her proposal for their kitchen and only asked that instead of a slider leading out to the deck that she have a French door installed, which required only a minor change to her plans. They'd even been flexible with their timetable, willing to wait until the end of the month for the work to begin. As a result, Addie was out of her office and in the private elevator up to Trent's apartment less than two hours after he left her office.

The moment she walked into the lobby of his building the

doorman recognized her and ushered her to the elevator that only accessed Trent's floors. On her previous visit she hadn't noticed that Trent used a special passcode to activate the elevator, but as it carried her up toward his floor it made sense to her. Trent's apartment took up the top two floors of the building. No one else needed access to those floors.

When the elevator stopped, the doors opened with a ding. Before stepping onto the gleaming floor in the foyer, she smoothed down her skirt. Thanks to the blended materials the skirt resisted wrinkles for the most part, but even so after wearing it all day a few were visible.

The sound of her heels on the tiles echoed in the silent space, and she took a moment to appreciate the beauty around her. Whoever designed and decorated the building made certain every part of it looked gorgeous, not just the apartment itself.

Ringing the bell, Addie waited for Trent to answer. When several minutes went by and he didn't answer, she reached into her purse for her cell phone. It made sense that in a place like this everything would be kept in working order, but things did break. Maybe the doorbell wasn't working or he hadn't heard it. From memory she dialed Trent's cell phone, but before she hit send the door swung open and Addie forgot her name.

"Sorry, I was in the shower when you rang the doorbell," Trent said, dressed in nothing more than a faded pair of jeans, his hair wet and his feet bare. "Come on in." He took a step back and pulled the door open wider.

Addie unglued her feet from the floor and took a step forward, unable to look away from the tiny drops of water on his chest and stomach. She'd seen plenty of pictures of gorgeous men with bodies like Trent's in magazines and on television but never in person. As if her hand had a mind of its own, she reached out and wiped away a droplet of water near his nipple.

"I'm glad your meeting didn't take long." One of his hands covered hers while the other pulled her closer.

Before he could say anything else, she pressed her lips against his, the instigator of their kiss for a change. "So do you always answer your door dressed like this?" she asked, pulling back from their kiss.

Trent gathered both her hands in his and raised them toward his mouth for a kiss. "Only when I know it's you," he said, the warmth of his smile echoing in his voice.

The warm kiss he placed on her hand traveled up her arms and throughout her body. "I bet you say that to all the women who show up on your doorstep." She kept her voice light and teasing.

"You're the first woman, other than my sister and cousin, to ever be here." He looked right at her as he spoke.

There was no mistaking the tingle of excitement that leapt to life at his words. With her hand still locked in his, Trent led her away from the door. "Make yourself comfortable while I grab a shirt." He stopped next to the sofa in the main living room.

You don't need to do that on my account. Addie nodded and watched him walk back toward the stairs that led up to the bedrooms on the second floor. Rather than sit, she wandered toward the windows overlooking the city. All day the sky had been gray. Despite the ominous weather predicted, the rain and thunderstorms hadn't made an appearance. Now though, the sky appeared darker than it should and, judging by the trees below, the winds had picked up. Wind and rain she could handle. It was the thunder and lightning that scared her.

UPSTAIRS TRENT GRABBED the first T-shirt his hand landed on. All week he'd looked forward to seeing Addie again and not because Marty insisted he keep to the timetable he'd set. In fact, he'd pushed Marty's plan to the back of his mind. Only after his conversation with the advisor that week had it made an unpleasant appearance and kept him from sleeping.

Instead, he looked forward to spending time with Addie for the simple reason that he liked her. He enjoyed their conversations both in person and on the phone. She made him laugh. Unlike other women he'd dated, she never put any pressure on him. Not once had she demanded to see him. She'd accepted and understood that he had work obligations during the week. Addie never sucked up to him either. When she didn't agree with him, she let him know. She even attempted to convince him to see things her way. And now after a long week, he had her all to himself. When he left for his meeting in Hartford that morning, he resigned himself to the fact he wouldn't see Addie until tomorrow. However, when his last meeting ended early, the only thing he'd been able to think about was getting back to Providence early enough to see her. Her agreement to stop by after her own meeting only sweetened the day.

"Not much to see out there tonight," Trent said when he re-entered the living room and found Addie by the windows. "Usually you get a great view of the sunset from that window." Trent stopped behind her, wrapped his arms around her waist, and pulled her against him.

As if they'd done it a hundred times before, she rested her head against him and placed her own hands over his. With the simple action, a sense of pure contentment struck him and he envisioned them standing like that every night watching the sunset over the city.

"I'd love to see it sometime."

She'd made a clear statement, but he detected the question in her voice. "You will." He didn't want there to be any doubts in her mind as to his intentions. "You'll enjoy the sunrises from up here, too." If she hadn't been in his arms, he would've missed that she held her breath for a moment at his mention of sunrises. "Since there's not much to see out there tonight, why don't we find something else to do? We can put on a movie. Or if you're hungry we can see what's in the kitchen?"

Turning in his arms, Addie smiled at him. Then before he could make the first move she placed a gentle kiss on his mouth. Although gentle and over all too soon, the single kiss warmed his very soul, and Trent could do nothing but stare at her when she broke contact, his mind busy processing the change in his emotions.

"I'm not hungry, but go ahead and eat if you are. A movie sounds good, though."

Oh, he was hungry all right but not for food. He wanted her naked in his bed more than he wanted his next breath. However, that wasn't something you told a woman like Addie, at least he didn't think so. A statement like that might send her running all the way back to her own place. "I'm all set for now, but how about some wine?"

Trent took her by the hand and led her into the kitchen. After looking through his selections they settled on a Cabernet, and then he led her back to his entertainment room with its movie projector. Walking in, Trent pressed the button on the wall to lower the screen. "What kind of movie do you feel like? A comedy maybe?" he asked as he hit the button that controlled the shades on the windows.

On the other side of the room, Addie kicked off her heels and settled herself on the leather sectional that occupied most of one wall. "How about something with some suspense?"

Trent ran through his list of movies in his head. "Have you seen that thriller Mia Troy did? I bought it last month but haven't watched it." He heard the first onslaught of rain hit the windows as he sat down. Immediately, he recalled the weatherman's forecast for the evening and Addie's reaction the last time there had been a thunderstorm. "If not, I also just got Anderson Brady's last movie." As he spoke Trent pulled Addie closer.

She didn't hesitate to snuggle up to him as she folded her legs up on the sofa. "I saw *Heartbreaker* when it first hit the theaters," Addie said referring to Mia Troy's latest movie. "It was great. Let's watch that one."

Trent accessed his movie collection and in moments the opening credits appeared on the screen. "If you need anything just say the word." More content and relaxed than he could ever remember being, he settled in to watch the movie and hold Addie close. As the opening credits disappeared and the movie got underway, he heard the first rumble of thunder. At least he thought it was thunder. Glancing over at Addie, he checked her reaction, but her eyes remained fixed on the screen.

Assuming the noise had come from the movie, he turned his attention back to the screen just as another rumble reached his ears. Next to him Addie tensed, and he knew the sound hadn't come from the movie.

"They said we would get storms tonight," Addie said as another clap of thunder filled the room.

He squeezed her hand. "Look on the bright side, we're not stuck in an elevator this time." Maybe if he made her laugh it would help her relax.

Before she could answer, a clap of thunder filled the room, this one so loud it sounded as if a bomb had gone off in his apartment. Under his arm, Addie jumped, her head bumping into his. "Sorry," she said as she pulled away to look at him. "I know thunderstorms are usually harmless, but I still hate them." She moistened her lips with her tongue, the action making his mouth hunger for the taste of her again.

"We all have things that bother us." He lowered his head toward hers, set on satisfying his need to kiss her while at the same time distracting her from the storm outside.

"Even you?" she asked her voice softer now.

He stopped mere inches from her mouth. "Even me," he whispered before his lips descended on hers. Her lips were warm and sweet and at first he kept his kisses gentle, allowing himself to savor every moment. The longer they kissed the greater the fire inside him burned. When Addie pressed her breasts against him and parted her lips, he couldn't stop himself from thrusting his tongue inside to meet hers.

Outside, another boom of thunder crashed, echoing the thudding of his heart. Pulling his mouth away from Addie's, he trailed his lips down her neck and then back up to her earlobe. With his tongue he traced the outline of her ear, causing Addie to sigh. With slow movements, he retraced his steps, pausing once again at her lips and kissing her before working his way to her other ear. As he sucked on her earlobe, warm skin came in contact with his as Addie's hands slid under his T-shirt and up his back. At first her movements remained tentative, but when he once again pressed his mouth against hers, they became more confident. Like a wildfire devouring dry brush, desire overtook him, and Trent reached for the buttons on her top.

Without breaking their kiss, he undid each tiny button, eager to remove the barrier between them. When he got the last button undone, he pushed the top from her shoulders, tossed it on the floor and then pulled back. For a moment he stared in silence, his eyes taking in the sight before him. "Beautiful," he said as he reached out and slid her bra straps down her shoulders. When she opened her mouth as if to comment, he covered it with his again. Then he reached around her back and undid the hooks of her bra.

Overhead the lights flickered and thunder crashed again, but unlike before, Addie didn't flinch. Eager to get rid of another barrier, Trent pulled back and tugged off his own shirt. Before he pulled her against him again, he reached out, his hands moving down her bare arms before making their way up her rib cage to cover her breasts, which just barely fit in his hands. At the intimate contact, her nipples came to life under his hands and he couldn't stop himself from lowering his head to take one into his mouth. When she moaned, he switched to the other side as his erection begged for some attention from the beautiful woman in his arms.

Still uncertain just how far Addie wanted to go tonight, he lowered her onto the couch and then looked down at her, waiting for any sign he should stop. In response, her eyes met his, then traveled down his body, her hands following the trail they made, leaving a scorching fire behind on his skin. When her hand paused at his waistband, he assumed she'd reverse her path. Instead, she rubbed a hand down the front of his jeans before undoing the button. As she slid the zipper down, he held his breath, and when she slipped a hand inside and touched him, he groaned. For a moment he lost himself in the feel of her hand on him; then he reached for her wrist and pulled her hand free. Before they went any further he needed to get them upstairs. While he planned on marrying Addie, that didn't mean he needed any children complicating things right now. The only way to prevent that meant using protection, which was upstairs.

Trent stood and kissed her as he pulled her to her feet. He continued to kiss her all the way across the apartment, only stopping long enough for them to make it up the stairs. Once in his room, he retook her mouth as he walked her toward the bed, stripping her of her skirt along the way. Dressed in only her low cut lace panties, she knelt on the bed facing him and reached for his jeans as another clap of thunder sounded. Rather than flinch, she pushed his jeans down until they reached his knees. Once he freed his legs from the jeans, she wrapped her arms around his neck and pulled him onto the bed with her.

Content now that her skin touched his, Trent allowed Addie to remain in control and enjoyed her caress as her hands wandered down his back, across his ass and to the tops of his thighs. When she reached his legs she started a path back the way she came, only this time when she reached his hip, she slipped a hand between them and ran a single finger down his penis. The simple touch brought his already burning desire into an inferno stage. With one simple movement, he rolled off her enough to remove her panties and then grabbed a condom from his wallet on the nightstand.

"Damn, you're beautiful," Trent said, unable to look away from Addie as he tore the condom package open. "Absolutely perfect." He slipped the condom on, then covered her body again with his.

Addie embraced him. "I wouldn't say—" Before she finished, he covered her mouth with his, thrusting his tongue inside her mouth as he slid inside her.

"HAVE THUNDERSTORMS ALWAYS SCARED YOU?" Trent asked from next to her on the sectional in the entertainment room two hours later. After they'd made love they'd cuddled in bed until both their stomachs demanded food.

Addie shook her head and swallowed the grape in her mouth. "No, at least I don't remember them bothering me until I was eight." Her eyes followed his hand as he reached out and grabbed a square of cheese from the platter in front of them. As if they had a mind of their own her eyes traveled from his hand, up his arm and to his bare chest. When they'd left his room, he'd only pulled back on his jeans and she was rather happy about that fact.

"What happened when you were eight?" he asked before he bit into his food.

She glanced back at the movie as the memories resurfaced. "We moved back to Rhode Island when I was seven and my family bought this huge old farmhouse in Burrillville. The house had been built during the Civil War, and my dad planned to remodel it in his free time. Anyway, the night before I turned eight, there was a huge thunder and lightning storm. It woke me up it was so loud. Lightning struck the electrical wires attached to the house. At first we all just thought the power went out, but then my brother smelled smoke. By the time the firefighters got there the house was engulfed." Visions from that night played through her head. Even after all this time she could hear the sirens as the fire trucks approached and smell the smoke in the air as the fire devoured the old wood.

Trent touched her cheek. "That's terrible. Did anyone get hurt?"

Addie swallowed back the emotions bubbling up. "My dad suffered some burns on his arms because of me, but otherwise everyone got out okay."

"How could that have been your fault?"

Although she'd never change what she'd done that night, she still regretted the danger she put her dad in. "We all managed to get out of the house fine, but once outside I realized Hersey, my dog, hadn't followed me, so I ran back in to get her. When my dad realized what I did, he rushed in after me. I found Hersey hiding under my bed. By the time my dad got to us in my room, the stairs had caught on fire. We ended up going out my brother's bedroom window onto the porch roof below and then to the ground." She shivered at the memory of rushing down the hall toward Rock's bedroom, Hersey in her arms. "I have never seen my father so angry at me as that night once we were all safe. And I knew even then that it was a stupid thing to do, but I just couldn't leave her in there."

Trent took her hand and kissed it. Once again she shivered, but this time it had nothing to do with the unpleasant memories.

"If one of my children ever did something like that I'd react like your father, but I get why you did it."

Trent a father, now that made quite the vision. With no effort she could see him holding a little baby with sapphire blue eyes and dirty blond hair

"What happened after?"

"We lived with my aunt and uncle for a little while, and my

parents had a new house built where the old one had been. They still live there."

Without any warning he scooped her up and sat her on his lap, the hem of the T-shirt she'd borrowed riding up her thigh. "And you've hated thunderstorms ever since," he said as more a statement than a question.

"Pretty much. If I'm tired enough sometimes I'll sleep through them, but otherwise they always make me jumpy."

"I think we just discovered another way for you to make it through a storm without it bothering you." Trent's hand slid up her bare thigh and under the hem of the T-shirt as he kissed her neck.

Addie laughed. "Then I guess whenever a storm is predicted I'll make sure you're close by." She placed a hand on his chest. Beneath her fingers she felt the muscles move as he continued his caress on her thigh.

"Now that sounds like an excellent idea." He moved in toward her as if to kiss her just as she turned her head and yawned. "Tired?"

"You could say that," she answered, uncovering her mouth. "I'm sorry. It's been a busy week."

Trent's hand slipped out from under her shirt and went around her waist. "No need to apologize. Why don't you spend the night here with me? Tomorrow we can go back to your place so you can get clean clothes."

She'd never spent the night at a man's house, let alone a man she'd known less than a month. Even so, the idea of falling asleep and waking up in Trent's arms was something she couldn't pass up. "Sounds perfect."

TEN

ADDIE PULLED at the cotton sheet, but it refused to budge. Yanking a little harder, she managed to move it a little further up her body. How could the thing be stuck? There was nothing in or near her bed for the sheet to get trapped by. Opening her eyes she caught a glimpse of the windows, which covered much of one wall. Heavy curtains covered them, blocking out much of the sunlight, but enough seeped in so Addie could see. Confused, she blinked a few times. This wasn't her room or her bed. Sitting up, she saw Trent's legs tangled in the sheets, and she remembered everything. With a smile her eyes made a path up his bare legs across his naked torso and to his face. His eyes were closed and the corners of his lips curved upward as if in a smile.

Careful not to wake him, she leaned forward and placed a light kiss on his mouth, then climbed out of bed. She'd never fall back to sleep now, but that didn't mean he had to get up. While she waited for him, she'd grab some coffee.

It took Addie a few minutes to figure out just how to use the fancy-looking coffee machine on Trent's kitchen counter. The thing had more buttons and switches than the inside of her car.

Thanks to the directions she found in a drawer, she managed to brew herself a perfect cup of coffee. But before she sat down and enjoyed it, she heard the muffled beep of her cell phone. Turning back into the kitchen, she grabbed the phone from her purse. Sure enough she'd missed three calls, and as she held the phone a text message popped up on the screen.

I'm at your house, where are you? the message from her cousin read. *I'm getting worried about you.* Since she'd moved into the condo, Chloe often stopped by unannounced, especially on the weekends if neither of them were scheduled to work. In fact, Chloe had her own key. And not once in the two years she'd lived there had Chloe ever stopped by and found the place empty. *Please call me*, the next message read. With the likelihood that Trent would wake up at any moment, she didn't want a long drawn out conversation with her cousin. If she told Chloe she'd spent the night with Trent, that was exactly what would happen. At the same time she wanted Chloe not to worry about her. Maybe if she kept her answers vague enough, she could reassure her cousin and keep the conversation short.

Addie put her coffee down and took a seat at the table. Then before her cousin called the police and reported her missing, she dialed her cell phone.

"Where the heck are you?" Chloe skipped the normal pleasantries when she answered. "I got here an hour ago. I've been calling your phone and the office. You never see clients this early so what are you up to?"

"I'm with a friend. Don't worry I'm fine."

"Then why didn't you answer any of my calls?"

"I was"—Addie paused, about to say asleep, then changed her mind—"didn't hear it." A tiny white lie like that never hurt anyone and as far as little lies went it wasn't that bad. After all, she hadn't heard the phone ring.

"Oh."

"Is something wrong?" Addie asked before her cousin could question her exact whereabouts.

"There's a picture of you and Trent outside Lucerne on the cover of *The Star Report*. Did you know that?" Chloe asked, the worry in her voice now replaced by excitement. "And inside there is a two-page spread of pictures of the two of you together. You didn't tell me you've been seeing him."

She hadn't meant to keep her relationship with Trent a secret from her cousin, but at the same time she hadn't gone out of her way to tell her either. "I told you I was doing some projects for him." She had shared at least that much.

"Please," Chloe said, drawing out the word. "There's a picture of you two together at WaterFire and his arms are around you. No client, not even Trent Sherbrooke, holds business associates like that. Now spill it."

Addie ignored her cousin's demand. "What other pictures are in there anyway?" She hadn't seen the sedan again since the night she and Trent enjoyed dinner at Lucerne and hadn't thought anymore about it. Had its owner been a photographer, and if so why hadn't she seen the car since?

"There's one of you exiting his office building and another of you two having coffee together. Then there is one of him heading inside your house. The article speculates on how you two met and the status of the relationship between you."

The picture of her and Trent that first time in the bakery had made her uncomfortable, but at least it had been in a very public place. The idea that pictures had been taken outside her home and office angered her.

"So is any of it true? Have you "Caught the Eye of Billionaire Playboy Trent Sherbrooke" like the headline says?" Chloe asked, quoting the article's headline.

What a stupid headline. Who came up with them anyway? "I'll tell you everything later. Promise."

"Come on, Addie," Chloe said, and Addie could imagine her cousin rolling her eyes. "This is me. I won't say anything to anyone."

More like sisters than just cousins, they'd always shared even the most personal information with each other. However, now wasn't the time or place to share. "We've been"—Addie stopped and searched for the most appropriate word choice—"spending time together."

"I can see that."

"Good morning." At Trent's greeting, Addie spun around and watched him enter the room.

"Chloe, I'll call you later tonight. I promise, okay," she said as she stood.

"You're with him now, aren't you?" Chloe asked, and Addie heard the smile in her voice. "Call me as soon as you can. I want all the details."

The line went dead before Addie said another word.

"Everything okay?" Trent wrapped his arms around her.

Leaning into his embrace, she encircled her arms around his waist, his bare skin warm against hers. "Chloe got worried when she stopped by my house and I wasn't home." Addie reached up and kissed his cheek, the facial hair that had grown in during the night rough against her lips.

Trent mimicked the kiss on her cheek, but then dropped an additional one on her lips. "I hope you told her you'll be unavailable all weekend." He moved his head and kissed her other cheek.

"Oh, am I?" She pulled back enough to look up at him.

"Yes, you are," he answered, kissing her between each word.

"Well, if you insist, I guess I can hang around." She tried to sound put out but the smile on her face ruined it.

He kissed her one last time before he moved to the coffeemaker on the counter and poured himself a mug. "Does your cousin always stop by like that?"

Her eyes fixated on his biceps as he raised the coffee to his mouth. Although well–defined, they'd didn't bulge out in that disgusting manner most body builders strived for. She let her eyes linger there before meeting his eyes. "A fair amount, especially if she wants to talk, like this morning." Should she mention the magazine or would he already know? Did he even care? The last published photo of them hadn't bothered him.

"This is the best coffee I've ever had out of that machine. Usually it's either as weak as dish water or strong enough to burn a hole in my stomach."

"I read the instructions someone left in the drawer."

Trent took another sip from his coffee. "I didn't know those were here."

Men. They were all the same when it came to directions. They all believed they were unnecessary. "Trent," Addie began, dismissing the coffee machine from her thoughts, "did you know there's a picture of us on the cover of *The Star Report Magazine*?"

In response he shrugged, then pulled out a kitchen chair and gestured for her to sit. "No, but who cares?"

She cared. He might be on magazine covers all the time, but she wasn't. "Chloe said there is a whole set of pictures inside with an article."

"That doesn't surprise me. It'll probably happen again, but after a while we'll be old news." He sat down next to her. "Don't worry about it."

Something between annoyance and anger descended on her. "Some of the pictures were taken outside my house."

"Do you remember the sedan you saw around the neighborhood? Turned out he was a freelance photographer." Trent covered her hand on the table with his.

He'd promised to look into it, but when she hadn't seen the car around anymore she didn't bother to ask. "I haven't seen the car in a while."

"My lawyer spoke with him. He explained that if he didn't stop stalking you, that you were going to press charges."

A part of her said she should be angry by his interference. The other was just relieved the photographer no longer hung around.

"I can't promise there won't be others at least for a little while, but they will go away. I should have warned you in the beginning, but it didn't occur to me." He leaned forward and kissed her. "Please don't let it change things between us."

The worry on his face looked out of place. "It doesn't, and I should have thought of it myself. I've been seeing pictures of you plastered on magazine covers forever." Addie only considered her words after they left her mouth and Trent glanced away. "Do you think there'll be a lot of other photographers?" His answer wouldn't change anything, but she wanted to know what to expect.

"For a little while, yes. If it'd make you feel better I can hire a bodyguard to keep an eye on you. If someone gets too close or gives you a hard time they'd handle it."

A bodyguard following her would be even worse than a photographer hanging around. "No, don't do that. I'll be fine."

"Are you sure? I want you to be safe." His voice echoed the worry still on his face.

"Positive. Besides, my dad is a retired Marine and I have four older brothers, so trust me, I know how to take care of myself. They all made sure of that."

Trent pulled her onto his lap. "If you change your mind, let me know."

Addie agreed, assuming it would make him feel better. After all, he didn't know she'd learned karate and boxing alongside her brothers or that she could shoot a gun better than most police officers. "How about we talk about something more pleasant? Like what we should do today."

Any residual concern faded from Trent's face and he gave her a look hot enough to boil water. "I have a few ideas." He slipped his hand under her T-shirt, his fingers closing around her breast. Her entire body tingled from the intimate contact and she sighed as her eyes closed. He massaged her breast until its nipple was taut and then transferred his hand to her other breast. As he repeated the process, he kissed her neck until he reached her earlobe. "My shirt looks good on you, but it would look even better on the floor," Trent said, his voice low but filled with desire. Before she could respond, his hand fell away and he reached for the hem of the T-shirt. In one fluid movement he pulled the shirt up and over her head, leaving her naked in his lap.

Of its own accord her body leaned toward him, eager for the feel of his skin against hers, but Trent dropped a hand on her shoulder stopping her. Without a single word his eyes dropped from her face to her breasts, and down across her torso before he repeated the caress and met her eyes again. "Much better," he said, his words stoking the fire already growing inside her. His hand once again left her shoulder and took possession of her breast. Unable to look away, she watched as he dipped his head, taking her nipple in his mouth.

Addie's eyes drifted closed, as his tongue teased her and sent a shudder of pleasure through her body. "I like your ideas," she said in a voice she almost didn't recognize.

Trent lifted his head and whispered, his breath warm against her skin, "I thought you might." Without another word he took her opposite nipple into his mouth and repeated the treatment on the other side. As he sucked and caressed her breast, Addie slid her hand down his stomach, his abs contracting under her hand until she reached the waistband of his shorts. She paused for a heartbeat then let her hand dip inside and wrap around his erection. The moment she touched him, Trent groaned, making her more confident. With slow, even movements she stroked her hand up and down his hot flesh until his hand clamped down over hers. "Let's go in the other room," he said and she heard the urgency in his voice.

"Your ideas keep getting better and better," she teased, a little breathless. Freeing her hand from under his, she stood and ignored the fact she was naked.

Rather than respond with words, Trent came to his feet, then in one motion grabbed her hand and headed for the stairs.

TRENT STOPPED in front of the bookcase in the cozy living room. The top shelf held pictures of Addie and her family. The smallest was of just her and her parents at her college graduation judging by the family resemblance. The one next to it was a wedding picture. Dressed in a floor-length deep purple gown, Addie stood next to a bride and groom in a Marine uniform along with two other men also in uniform, who shared a family resemblance. The final picture featured Addie and the same men from the wedding picture as well as another man. In this picture, though, they were all dressed casually and joined by a couple he suspected were her grandparents. The rest of the shelves were filled with books on architecture and DVDs. Magazines about decorating and travel sat on the small coffee table along with a notebook and pen. Other than the magazines, the entire room remained neat with everything in its own place. He'd noticed the same thing about the small kitchen when he'd last stopped at Addie's house. Unless she hid all of her clutter in her bedroom, Addie liked everything neat and well organized, much like him.

He'd never before considered how a girlfriend preferred her home. If they liked it cluttered with various trinkets and expensive toys that was their business, it didn't affect him one way or the other. Now, however, standing in Addie's living room while she showered and dressed, it pleased him to see she liked to keep her house much like he did. Not that he needed anything else to endear her to him. Already he found himself attracted to her and not just physically. Somehow in the short time they'd known each other, she'd become important to him in a way he'd never experienced before. When they weren't together he missed her. During their phone conversations he shared the details of his day, something he'd never done with a woman before her. The women he'd dated in the past hadn't cared how his meeting had gone or whether or not he had a good night's sleep. They'd been more concerned with what hot, exotic vacation spot he planned to whisk them off to or what new piece of jewelry he'd purchased for them. Addie made no such demands on him. Instead, she asked him questions about himself, his likes and dislikes or how he felt at the moment. In return, he used their conversations to get to know more about her and not just the things he'd already learned from Marty's file. Thanks to their conversations he knew she'd once dyed her hair bright pink and that when she was six she fell off her bike and knocked out her two front baby teeth.

Yup, he cared about Addie in a way he'd never thought possible. The fact should've thrilled him, considering Marty's plan, and in a way it did. Now that he started this relationship with her, he could easily imagine marrying her. Yet, every time he thought of that a heavy dose of guilt punched him in the stomach. Even though his emotions were involved now, he'd started their relationship with his own personal gains in mind. If the tables were reversed he'd be furious if someone did the same to him and he learned the truth.

She's not going to find out. He reminded himself again. Besides, what he felt now was genuine, so regardless of why he started things, he cared about her now.

"You could have sat down," Addie said as she entered the

room, her wet hair pulled back in a ponytail, leaving a wet spot on her T-shirt.

Unfamiliar happiness took him by surprise, and he said a little thank you to fate for placing Addie in his path that day outside the bakery. "I was looking at your pictures." He tilted his head toward the bookshelf. "I'm guessing those are your brothers."

Addie walked around him and took one picture from the shelf. "We had a sixtieth wedding anniversary for my grandparents a few years ago. I don't know how but all my brothers made it." She pointed first to the older couple in the front. "These are my mom's parents." Next, she pointed to the man on her left. "This is Tom, he's three years older than me. Jon, who is next to my grandfather, is the oldest. He's seven years old than me. Frank is behind my grandmother. There are only ten months between him and Jon." She pointed to each man as she spoke. "Rock is a year and half older than me. I've always been closest to him." She put the picture back on the shelf. "I don't think we've all been together again like that since then."

As much as he and his siblings did their own things and went their own ways, they still tried to get together at least once a year regardless, if only for a few hours. "That must be hard on your parents."

"A little, but they get it, especially my dad." She moved back across the room toward the doorway. "I'm going to grab a glass of iced tea. Would you like some?"

"Sounds good and we can decide how to spend the rest of the day." He followed her into the kitchen, which like the rest of the house was tidy. The roses he'd brought her on their first date remained in a vase on the counter although they'd started to wilt. "Looks like I need to get you new roses." He stopped next to the flowers and pulled one from the vase, his eyes spotting the handwritten schedule.

"I loved the flowers, but you don't have to get me anything." She handed him a tall glass of iced tea.

Her statement reinforced what he already knew. Addie was nothing like the women from his past. "I know." Trent kissed her before he took a sip from his drink. "What's this?" He pointed to the schedule on the counter.

"My hours at the bakery next week." She walked away and took a seat at the table.

He scanned the hours printed on the paper, adding them up in his head. "You're scheduled for twenty hours next week. Do you always work that much?" When Marty told him she worked part time at the bakery, he'd assumed that meant eight or nine hours not twenty.

Addie paused, her own glass almost to her mouth. "More or less."

No wonder she'd been tired last night. She must work close to seventy hours a week. "Do you need to work that much?" he asked, confident he knew the answer. Assuming she made at least minimum wage, twenty hours a week at the bakery would bring in a little more than six hundred dollars a month

She nodded. "Most of what Designs by Addison makes goes back into the business and until recently business had been on the slow side. The money from the bakery helps with my personal expenses." Her tone remained neutral not giving him any hint of how she felt about her situation. "If things stay the way they have been, though, I should be able to cut back at the bakery soon."

Concern for her well being filled him. A person, no matter their age or health, could only sustain a sixty-plus-hour workweek for so long before it started affecting them. "How can I help?"

"Help? You already have. Ever since you hired me to redecorate your office and work on your house, my business has exploded. I don't need you to do anything."

He recognized the look of determination on her face, but it didn't stop him. "I realize you don't need it." He picked his words carefully as he went on. "Trust me, I have my own selfish reasons for wanting to help you." Trent took her hand. "The less time you work, the more time you can spend with me. So you see by helping you, I'm really helping myself."

Addie rolled her eyes. "So the truth comes out," she said with a little laugh. "Really, Trent, I'm fine. Besides, other than dragging clients into my office by their hair, which would be really bad if you plan to run for Senate, there isn't anything you can do."

"Yeah, that would be bad." Even as he agreed, he searched his brain for ways to help her. Even without asking he knew she would never accept his money, and he couldn't exactly buy stock shares in her company.

"Honestly, Trent. I'm fine and I promise to make plenty of time for you. Don't worry about it."

The smile on her lips called to him. Later when he was alone he'd think of something. Right now, though, he planned to just enjoy their afternoon together. "I'm going to hold you to that." He moved closer and dropped a kiss on her forehead. "So how do you want to spend the day?" According to her work schedule she only had today off. The following day she was scheduled from eight until two. "I'll go anywhere you want."

Addie didn't hesitate. "If you don't mind, I'd love to visit the Museum of Fine Arts in Boston. They have a visiting exhibit of paintings by Caravaggio," she said, referring to the Italian artist who had painted during the late 1500s. "The paintings are only there for a few more weeks."

He'd already guessed she enjoyed art given the framed replicas she had on her walls. In all honesty, a day at the art museum didn't sound as much fun as a day out on his cousin's sailboat, which Jake kept moored in Newport, but if that was how she wanted to spend the day, he'd go along.

"If you don't want to drive into Boston today, that's okay. We can do something else."

"I don't mind. Traffic should be light today and the MFA has some great collections." His reply earned him a smile, which was reward enough for a day spent in a museum. Ten minutes later, they headed out. Addie could spend the day studying old paintings while he studied her.

ELEVEN

Monday afternoon Addie fought back yet another yawn, then reached for the energy drink she'd grabbed on her way into work. The weekend had been as wonderful as the one before, but it had drained her. Between her late night with Trent on Friday and Saturday, she got nothing else done before her afternoon shift on Sunday. In order to catch up, she'd worked late Sunday night on paperwork so that today she could focus on the decorating plans for a new client and put some more work into her design plans for Trent's house in Newport. Both goals she wanted accomplished before she left for the night. Tomorrow she had an appointment with a potential client out on Cape Cod and doubted she'd make it into the office at all. For that reason she'd asked Tara to work the next day so that the office would remain open.

Finishing the drink in a few sips, she focused once again on her computer screen. The window treatments she'd found from one of her favorite manufacturers matched the sofa the clients insisted upon. Unfortunately, they clashed with the wall paint she planned to propose. Unless she wanted to change the paint color, she needed to find something else. So far the only other window treatments she'd found that worked were floor-length curtains, which the clients had specifically stated they didn't want. With a sigh, Addie called up another manufacturer website she liked.

The office door opened and Tara stepped in as she scrolled through the various selections. "Addie, Marcy Blake is here to see you." Tara crossed to her desk and dropped a business card in front of her. "She's from *Today Magazine*."

She'd never heard of the woman, but she'd both heard of and read *Today Magazine*. At one time she'd even had a subscription to the popular monthly magazine, which ran articles on everything from celebrities to important news stories. Just last month it had featured the story of how a family survived for three months on an uninhabited island after their boat went astray in the Pacific Ocean.

"Thanks, Tara. Send her in." As Tara left, Addie scanned her desk, moving anything with a client name or address into a drawer.

A moment later the door opened again and a stylish dark-haired woman entered. "Thank you for seeing me, Addison. I hope this isn't a bad time."

Was there ever a good time to talk to reporters? "No, it's fine. Please have a seat." Addie folded her hands before her as Marcy placed her leather bag on the floor and sat.

Marcy gave her a wide smile as she focused all her attention on her. "I'm sure you know why I'm here."

Addie nodded. Trent warned her that the other magazine article about them wouldn't be the last. Even still, the reporter's visit today surprised her.

"Trent Sherbrooke has well established his reputation as a playboy going from one model or socialite to another. He even dated a Danish princess for a few months." The reporter told her things she already knew but had tried not to think about. "And then all of a sudden you, a small business owner, show up on his arm. People are intrigued. They want to know all the details."

She wanted to squirm under the reporter's gaze, which made her feel like a bug under a microscope. Clearing her throat instead, Addie said, "There's not much to tell."

Marcy waved a hand, the bangle bracelets on her arm clinking together. "When it comes to someone like Trent Sherbrooke, there's always a lot to tell. How about we start with how you two met?"

Her gut instinct was to tell the reporter it was none of her business. Whatever happened between her and Trent concerned only them. But she'd read enough magazine articles to know when it came to well-known public figures, that wasn't always the case. In fact, not long ago she'd read an article about Trent's cousin Sara after she announced her engagement to billionaire Christopher Hall. So unless she wanted the reporter to make stuff up, she'd better answer. "We met by accident. He bumped into me on Benefit Street outside Ambrosia Pastry Shop and Cafe one afternoon."

Marcy placed a MP3 recorder on the desk and switched it on. "Is that when the picture of you two together that appeared in the *Providence Gazette* was taken?" As she spoke, she pulled a notepad with questions from her bag.

The woman came prepared. Addie eyed the long list of questions on the pad. Judging by the length, they were going to be there for a while.

For over an hour Marcy asked questions that spanned from how they met to whether or not she'd met his family. She'd even gone so far as to ask if they'd discussed moving in together yet. Throughout the interview Addie reminded herself that it was better for both of them if she answered rather than let Marcy speculate and fabricate some kind of story. Of course, she realized that even by answering the questions that didn't mean Marcy wouldn't concoct something of her own anyway.

Wasn't that something celebrities complained about all the time?

"Thank you for answering my questions today, Addison. I appreciate your cooperation."

Addie forced a smile as she watched the reporter return her belongings to her bag. "Anytime, Marcy."

Slipping the leather strap from her briefcase onto her arm, Marcy stood, her Cheshire cat smile on her face again. "I wish you all the best of luck with Mr. Sherbrooke. Maybe you'll be the one to finally tame him. Just because a princess couldn't doesn't mean you can't."

At the reporter's comment fear twisted around her heart, but Addie made herself smile. "Thank you. Have a nice day."

She kept the smile on her face until the office door closed behind the reporter. Once alone again she sagged back into her chair and blew out a slow deep breath. Even before their brief run-in on the sidewalk that day, she'd known about Trent's reputation. That didn't mean she liked to think about it or what it meant for their future together. Rather, she preferred to enjoy their time together, getting to know the real him. And while much of what she read about him was true, there was so much more to him. He had goals that he wanted to accomplish that no magazine ever wrote about. He enjoyed hanging around and just watching movies with her. He hated country music but listened to it anyway in the car with her because she liked it. And no matter what, Trent was always polite and considerate. Not once since they'd started dating had he put his own personal preferences first. Magazine articles never mentioned any of those things. Things that she loved about him.

Addie didn't even pause as the word love materialized in her thoughts. They hadn't known each other all that long, but already her heart had become engaged in their relationship. She'd never fallen so hard so fast for a guy. With her last relationship, they'd known each other for more than a year as friends before ever going on their first date. Even then their relationship remained casual for the first few months of dating. Only after five or so months had they committed themselves to a long-term relationship that in the end lasted for two years.

Nothing about this thing with Trent resembled that relationship or any of her others. She missed him like crazy when they were apart. When they were together they didn't need to do anything special. She enjoyed sitting in his arms and talking. As far as she could tell he enjoyed it, too. He never insisted they go out. In fact, if she hadn't read otherwise in countless magazine articles she'd guess he hated clubs and parties.

And if you hope to see him tomorrow, you better get back to work. Addie hit a key on her keyboard and the screen came to life again. Yup, she'd save the dreams for tonight when she climbed into bed.

———

TRENT LEANED back in his office chair and looked around, once again amazed at the transformation. The ideas, which looked good on Addie's computer screen weeks ago, appeared even better in reality. She'd turned the lackluster space into a personal sanctuary, a place almost as inviting and comfortable as his own home. If she'd done that to this space, he couldn't wait to see the end results to his home in Newport.

Already he pictured the two of them in the kitchen she'd designed sharing breakfast while they enjoyed the ocean view. She'd promised to have the final designs for the bathrooms ready for tomorrow night. Whether she managed it or not didn't matter to him. All he cared about was seeing her. It'd only been a little more than a day since she left his apartment Sunday morning and gone to work at the bakery, but his body claimed it was much longer. After two nights falling asleep with her cuddled close, he'd had trouble falling asleep the night before without her. Then when he'd woken that morning alone, his apartment seemed cold and empty. Tomorrow morning it would be the same way.

There's one way to fix that. The thought jumped into his head. If she moved in he'd fall asleep with her next to him every night and see her every morning. Not only that, but if she moved in she'd have money and perhaps quit the bakery. Asking her would benefit both of them. His mood brightened at the thought.

But was it too soon? He'd never asked a woman to move in with him. Was there an appropriate time frame for that sort of thing? And if he did ask, would she agree? The initial confidence toward the idea dimmed. Before he jumped in and did something unwise, he better think about it.

Across the room, a knock sounded on the door just before it opened and Marty Phillips entered for their scheduled appointment. "Judging by those photos in *The Star Report Magazine*, you're making great progress with Addison." Marty dropped his briefcase on the conference table. "Excellent work."

He almost told the advisor to shut his mouth, but he managed to keep silent. Instead, he took a seat across from Marty, ready to work.

"A source of mine at *Today Magazine* informed me the chief editor sent Marcy Blake out to interview her."

This time no amount of self-control could hold back his groan. Marcy Blake was well known for her celebrity pieces. In fact, she'd done multiple ones on his cousins Jake and Sara in the past, both times manipulating or plain old making up facts so the stories were juicer.

"But before we get into the specifics of your relationship, I want to focus on your likely competition as of now." Marty pulled a laptop from his brief case. "I know for a fact Daniel Potter has hired Roberta Featherton as his advisor. In case you haven't heard of her she worked on Governor Wentworth's campaign and Senator Lockhart's."

While not well, he knew Daniel Potter. They'd attended Harvard for a year together; Daniel had been a senior the year Trent started.

"Potter possesses no political experience either," Marty continued. "However, he does have a wife of three years and a one-year-old daughter. As of yet I've been unable to uncover anything that would tarnish his reputation, but I have people digging."

Trent doubted Marty's search would dig anything up. The Daniel Potter he remembered was a decent guy if not a bit full of himself.

Marty powered up his laptop. "Of course he doesn't have the same financial resources as you or the same family clout." When the screen lit up he brought up a file and then pushed the laptop off to the side. "I've also heard, although it hasn't been confirmed, that Harry Thatcher intends to run as an independent. Thatcher himself isn't a concern, but he might pull just enough votes away from you, allowing Potter to win."

Trent agreed. There was next to no chance that Thatcher could win. He'd run in the past two elections and lost. His entry into the race as a third party candidate, however, could affect his own chances at election. "What are the chances he'll run?"

"Not sure. I've heard a rumor from another source that his health is failing. If that's true, a run for Senate might be too much for him. We'll have to keep an eye on things." Marty paused for a drink of water. "Now there are some upcoming functions you need to attend. I've prepared a spreadsheet for you listing them in order of importance, who'll be in attendance that you need to connect with, and when they are. I've already procured the necessary invites. I need you to decide which ones fit your current schedule." He turned the laptop so Trent could see the screen. "The Charity Auction for the Providence Children's Hospital is in my opinion the most imperative at present. Agatha Beland, Vincent Beland's wife, is on the board of directors and this is her baby. She oversees this auction every year."

Trent recognized the name. Vincent Beland, a former Rhode Island governor and wealthy businessman, remained well respected in Rhode Island politics.

"In the past five years no candidate with Beland's backing has lost an election. You want him on your side."

As Marty spoke, Trent scanned the list of various events ranging from fundraisers to house parties. For now, he'd commit to the hospital fundraiser. Later he'd go through the list in more detail and pick and choose what events he and Addie wanted to attend. "I'll take care of this before the weekend is over."

"I emailed you a copy already. Now let's discuss your personal life. I'm pleased to see you've kept away from other women, or at least haven't been seen with any. And thus far the media has only had positive things to say about your relationship with Addison."

At Marty's words, Trent's instincts went into defensive mode. The idea of discussing something so personal with the advisor left a sour taste in his mouth. Unfortunately, there wasn't any way around it. He'd just make sure to keep it from getting too personal. "We've been spending a lot of time together."

"Good. I assume that means you've moved past the just holding hands stage." Marty gave him a knowing look, and Trent ground his teeth together to keep from saying something he'd later regret.

In the past he'd shared the details of his sex life with friends, yet now Marty's question caused his anger to flare. The already present need to protect what he shared with Addie kicked itself up a few more degrees. "You don't need specific details. All you need to know is we're happy together," Trent answered his voice cool and controlled.

"In that case do you think we can manipulate the time table? Is a marriage proposal in the next two months or so possible?

Perhaps a wedding by spring—and who knows— maybe a baby on the way next year at this time when the real campaigning starts?"

He pictured Addie in his life on a permanent basis with no problem, but he despised the planned and calculated way Marty mapped it out. "I see no reason to rush everything." When his fingernail bit into his palm, Trent realized he'd clenched his fist and relaxed his hands. "Let's leave everything as planned."

Across the table Marty's eyes narrowed. "You hired me to win. The sooner you turn into a happily married man the better," Marty said, his southern drawl becoming more distinct. "And if there is the possibility of making you a happily married *family* man, all the better. Especially now that we know Potter will be your main competition."

He had hired Phillips because of his track record of getting candidates elected. Back then he hadn't considered the guy's methods, or Addison, for that matter.

"I don't see the problem. The end result will be the same anyway, you'll just make the trip down the aisle sooner rather than later." Marty's expression relaxed. "Either way, you still end up with the old ball and chain."

He'd never considered Marty's marital status, but judging by his words, the guy thought little of marriage. "Marty, I can't make any promises, but I'll think about it. Can we move on?"

The advisor looked displeased but perhaps realizing who wrote his paychecks, he nodded. "You need to convince Addison to leave the bakery soon. A potential United States Senator in Washington may have a girlfriend with a professional career, but not one who pours coffee as a part-time job."

Trent counted to ten before answering. "I have considered it, but not because I mind that she pours coffee," he said through clenched teeth.

"Whether you have a problem with it or not, other people

may not see it that way. You know as well as I do that politics is as much about image as it is about the issues."

It rubbed him the wrong way, but again Marty had hit the nail on the head.

"And she doesn't have to quit tomorrow, just soon."

His brain reverted back to the ideas he'd come up with over the past week to help her financially. "I'll work on it."

Marty gave him a stiff nod. "Okay, then I think we're all set for now unless you have any other questions for me." He powered down his laptop as he spoke.

"Just one. Any luck on who sent that first picture into the *Gazette*?" At this point he didn't care, but Addie had asked him about it again.

"Dead end. My contact at the paper insists she received the picture anonymously, but I have someone tracing the IP address it came from. Anything else?"

Coming to his feet, Trent extended his hand. "Nothing else now. I'll let you know which events Addie and I plan to attend."

After shaking his hand the advisor left, and Trent went back to his thoughts on helping Addie. Aside from her moving in with him, eliminating her housing costs, one idea stood out as an ideal solution. What if he gave her office space in this building? The lawyer on the fourth floor, a long-time leaser and friend of his father, had recently retired. He could offer her the space for free, but without even proposing the idea he knew she'd refuse. That didn't mean he couldn't offer the space for less than she paid now for rent. Not only would that help her financially, it would put her closer to him on a daily basis. If he did make the offer, he'd have to be careful of how he went about it. Before he said anything he'd have to consider his words and approach. In the meantime, he'd have Shirley contact the owner of Addie's building on Benefit Street and find out how much she paid for rent.

DRESSED in her favorite pj's, Addie dropped onto the couch and switched on the television. The week before most of her favorite television shows had returned from their summer break with new episodes and thanks to her DVR she could watch them now. First, she needed to decide what she was in the mood for. Did she want something funny or a drama? Then again she could try something new. A new paranormal series had debuted that weekend, and it looked interesting enough to give a try. Scrolling through her list of recorded shows, she read the short description of each episode, then settled on the new paranormal. Not interested in the opening credits, she hit the fast forward button until she arrived at the opening scene. But no sooner did the action begin, when her phone rang, the guitar chords from *Stairway to Heaven*, Trent's ringtone, filling the room. She'd set the special ringtone for him after their first official date weeks earlier.

"Hey, you," she said as she paused the television show on the screen, catching the actors in a ridiculous pose. "Are you already home?" She remembered that he'd had a late afternoon meeting with his campaign advisor that day followed by dinner with his father, stepmother, and one of his brothers who was in town.

"Just walked in," Trent answered as she pictured him climbing the stairs up to the second floor, pulling off his tie as he walked. "Everyone was disappointed that you didn't join us. They want to meet you."

When he'd invited her, the idea of meeting his family overwhelmed her. Heck, she'd once worked for his stepmother, not that the woman knew that. He'd understood when she'd declined, but if their relationship continued, at some point she might have to meet his family.

"And I want you to meet them."

Trent's words caused her heart to skip a beat. "Next time, I promise," she answered. "But with you not around, I finished all my work so tomorrow night I'm all yours."

"Good. Why don't you stay here tomorrow night? There's no reason you can't go to work from my place the next day."

She loved the idea of falling asleep and then waking up next to Trent. In fact, if she could do it every day she would. "I'll pack a bag before I leave here in the morning. I'm not sure what time I'll be back in the city. I have an appointment out on the Cape again tomorrow."

"Whenever you get here is fine. If I'm not here I'll leave instructions with Paul to let you in," Trent said, referring to the doorman who worked in the afternoons. "Marty told me Marcy Blake stopped in your office today. Are you okay?" Trent asked his concern coming through the phone.

For the next fifteen minutes she told him about her unexpected visit from the magazine reporter, including all the questions Marcy asked and the answers she'd given. As she did, she began to second-guess some of her answers, worried that she'd answered in such a way that the reporter might twist her words or print them in a negative way.

"Don't worry about it, sweetheart," Trent said, the endearment he used catching her full attention. In the past he'd called her Addison or Addie, this change drove home how serious their relationship had become. "I'm sure you did fine, but if she does print something wrong it's not your fault. That reporter could twist a simple yes into something else."

He'd intended his words to reassure her, but they had the opposite effect. Rather than complain and appear to be whining, she changed the subject altogether. "How did your meeting with Marty go?" She knew little about the man other than he'd worked on the President's campaign, which Trent had only told her after she asked how he'd found the advisor. While she knew such advisors existed, she didn't have the first clue as to how a potential politician went about finding such people to manage things.

In response, Addie only received silence. "Trent, are you still there?" she asked when she feared she'd lost the connection.

"Yeah, sorry. I dropped the phone taking off my shirt. My meeting went fine. He gave me a list of events I should attend. I thought we could go through it together and decide which ones to go to. For now, the only one I agreed to was the Annual Charity Auction for the Providence Children's Hospital. It's the first Saturday night in October. Can you make sure you have that night free?"

She'd heard of the event held at the Biltmore Hotel. Organized by a former governor's wife, it attracted celebrities and wealthy individuals from around the country. Over the years the money raised by the event had been used for everything from expanding the hospital to building nearby housing for families to stay in when their children were confined to the hospital for extended periods of time. "Will do." The next time she worked at the bakery, she'd put in for the whole day off. "Did he ever find out who sent that picture into the newspaper?"

"Not yet, but he's still working on it," Trent answered. "Let's talk about something besides my meeting with Marty."

She'd noticed before that he didn't like to talk about Marty, or politics, for that matter. Now, like before, she assumed it was his way of keeping work at the office. "Okay, what do you want to talk about?" As much as she enjoyed hearing about all aspects of his life, she could understand and respect his desire to not think about work once the day ended.

"How about our plans for the weekend? You're only working Friday night, right?"

The remainder of the conversation focused on the upcoming weekend and their plans.

TWELVE

IN THE WEEK and half since their last face-to-face meeting, Marty had called him twice and on both occasions he'd inquired about Trent's progress toward getting Addie to leave the bakery. Both times he'd assured the man he had everything under control, but in truth he'd been avoiding the topic with her. Tonight he'd address the issue, not only to get Marty off his ass but also because he wanted more of her time. While he realized that was a selfish reason for his actions, he just didn't care. He had the means to help her and make them both happy, why shouldn't he do it?

Opening his brief case, Trent made sure he had the lease agreement for the office space as well as the extra key to his apartment, which he planned to give Addie that night. Satisfied he had everything he required, he switched off his office lights and headed out. Traffic from Providence to Cumberland remained light as he took the 146 exit off Interstate 95 and headed north. As he drove, Trent considered the words he'd decided to use when he proposed the idea of moving her office. In the past, he'd always been confident of the outcome when he dealt with women, not so this time. He had no idea how she might respond.

Fifteen minutes after getting on 146, Trent took his exit and then turned onto Addie's street. The trees on both sides once full of bright green leaves now contained a few orange and red ones too as fall approached. In another few weeks the trees would showcase a mix of red, orange and yellow leaves before they all fell to the ground leaving a mess behind for homeowners. Some people hated this time of year. His sister always complained it signified the beginning of the end as the weather in New England changed and the temperatures began to drop. Trent loved each of the seasons New England offered, something other parts of the world didn't experience and he'd missed during the years he'd lived abroad. Maybe in the next few weeks, he'd make reservations for them up in Vermont. While the foliage around here was great, nothing compared to the colors up there.

Before getting out of the car, Trent grabbed the items he wanted from his briefcase stuck them inside his jacket pocket, then headed up the walkway. Since his last visit, she'd added some potted mums to her steps, another distinct sign of fall. Today the front door remained open and Mick Jagger's voice reached him from the other side of the screen door. Ringing the doorbell, he waited.

In a matter of seconds Addie appeared in the narrow hall that led into the kitchen, a dishtowel over her shoulder. "Come on in," she said before turning back into the kitchen.

Trent followed, the delicious smells emanating from the kitchen were stronger the further he walked in. "I wanted to surprise you, but I got home later than I intended," Addie said from in front of the stove. An off-white tablecloth covered the small kitchen table that was set for two, complete with wine glasses and candles. "Dinner needs about ten more minutes," she said as she lifted one lid and mixed its contents. "But the pasta e fagioli is ready." She pointed to the soup in the pot.

"Whatever you're cooking smells wonderful." Trent came up behind her, wrapped his arm around her and kissed her neck.

"Chicken cacciatore," she answered. "It's my grandmother's recipe. I hope you like it." She put down the wooden spoon and turned in his arms. "And I made zeppoles for dessert." She gave him a peck on the lips. "Have a seat." She walked around him toward the counter. "I already opened the wine."

He stood and watched her retrieve the bottle and then pour it. He'd never had a girlfriend cook him a meal. "You didn't have to do all this."

"I know, but I wanted to." Addie walked back to him and tugged his hand. "Now sit down so we can eat."

Trent did more eating than talking during dinner. The meal Addie prepared could only be described by one word—fantastic. She'd mentioned she'd gotten home later than intended, which meant she'd worked that day as well. He had no idea how she'd managed to prepare such an out of this world meal in such a short period of time. "I can't eat another bite," Trent said after he swallowed the last of his zeppole, the custard leaving a sweet taste in his mouth. "If I'd known you cooked like this, I would have started coming here every night for dinner weeks ago."

"You can stop by for dinner whenever you want, but most nights I don't cook much more than some leftover soup and a grilled cheese sandwich." She raised her own zeppole to her mouth and took a bite, some of the custard from inside lingering on her lips.

Before she wiped it away with a napkin, he leaned toward her and licked it away with his tongue. "Mmm, tastes almost as good as you," he said, intent on kissing her, but instead Addie laughed, stopping him dead in his tracks. "What's so funny?"

"You. You probably say that to all the women you kiss."

Only on one other occasion had she mentioned his past, which he appreciated. This time, however, he wanted her to know she wasn't like the women he'd dated in the past. "Whatever I said to other women in the past doesn't matter. Only you matter." Now seemed like the perfect opportunity to give her the key. "I want you to have something." He dug into the pocket of the jacket he'd tossed across his chair and pulled out the key. "You already have the elevator code, but I want you to have a key, too. That way you can come and go whenever you want, even if I'm not home."

Addie accepted the key, studying it as if it were a foreign object. "I'm not sure if I'll stop by if you're not there, but thank you." She stuck the key in her jeans pocket. "I have an extra key in my desk that you can have."

"I have something else for you," Trent said as he retrieved the lease agreement. "There's some office space available on the fourth floor of my building. I thought you might be interested in it."

Addie accepted the papers he held out but didn't unfold them; instead she dropped them on the table by her plate. "Trent, I can't afford the rent in your building. Besides, I have one more month on my current lease."

"You'll be able to afford it. Open the agreement." He picked it up and handed it to her again. Addie eyed him with suspicion but complied with his request. He watched as her eyes moved across the page and knew when she'd hit the line stating the monthly rate. Her eyes snapped to his.

"What is this? The rent isn't even half of what I pay now. Are you renting me a closet?" She folded up the agreement and then held it toward him. When he refused to take the papers back, she dropped them on the table again. "I can't accept this, Trent. Where I am now is fine, and my landlord agreed not to raise my rent if I sign another two -year lease."

Stubborn woman. "This is more for my benefit than yours. With you just a few floors down, I can see you whenever I want. And the lower rent will cut down business expenses so you can quit the bakery. Again, that means more time for me." He caressed the skin on her arm.

Addie stilled his hand with her own. "I appreciate the offer, Trent. Please don't think I don't, but I can't accept this."

Trent opened his mouth to reply, but she cut him off. "And don't try to tell me that is what everyone pays for rent in your building."

"Come on, Addie. What's the big deal? You get a bigger office and a little break on rent." He'd expected resistance if he offered her the space but assumed she'd come around. Her tone of voice and posture said otherwise.

"I don't want your charity, Trent. If my business is going to succeed I want it to be because of me, not because I got some special deal."

He admired her determination, but at the moment he wished she'd let it go a little. "Will you at least consider it?" he asked.

"If at some point I can afford the rent in your building, I'll be happy to move my office. Until then, I'll remain where I am."

Her tone told him she was done with the discussion. Out of ideas, he raked a hand through his hair. "Damn it, Addison. What good is having money if I can't use it to help the woman I love?" The words flew from his mouth with no conscious thought on his part, but once he said the words his brain kicked in as did his shock. He hadn't intended to say he loved her, heck, he'd never even thought it before now. With the words out there between them, he realized it was true. Addie had managed to do what no other woman ever had—worked her way into his heart.

Next to him, Addie's eyes remained wide and she sat motionless. Then, as if she'd just been sent back to her body, a small tentative smile formed on her face. "I love you, too." She bit down on her bottom lip before she spoke again. "Is this that important to you?"

Almost there. "I worry about you working so much, and I want you closer to me."

Addie picked up the lease agreement and scanned it again. "Okay, but I don't want any other special treatment in terms of this lease. If in two years when this lease is up everyone's rent goes up, I expect mine to go up as well."

"We can worry about that then," he answered. By that time she'd be his wife and money would no longer be an obstacle for her.

"Trent, I'm serious. I won't sign unless you agree." She crossed her arms across her chest and stared at him.

"Fine, as long as you quit the bakery as soon as possible. And just for the record, I don't like it."

Addie nodded. "I'll give my two week notice tomorrow when I go in."

Marty wanted it sooner than that, but it would have to do. Convincing Addie not to give a sufficient notice would never happen. "And I'll arrange to have your office moved." She opened her mouth prepared to argue, but he didn't give her a chance. "Since this is my idea, I'll pay for it. If it makes you feel better consider it partial payment for the work you're doing on my house." Trent pulled a pen from his jacket pocket. "Why don't you sign now and then show me the new designs you told me about?" He wanted it a done deal before she thought more about it and changed her mind.

Accepting the pen, she smoothed out the papers, her eyes reading them one last time. Trent watched as she touched the pen to the signature line, then paused and glanced up at him one more time. When she signed her name across the line, he let out the breath he hadn't realized he'd been holding.

"This will be good for both of us." Trent took back the papers. "Just think about the fun lunch breaks we can have together." His tone of voice let her know that those lunch breaks wouldn't involve any actual food. Once the agreement was safely back in his pocket, he moved toward her. "Maybe we should look at those designs before we get distracted with other activities, sweetheart." He kissed her, just a gentle press of his lips against hers.

Addie's entire face lit up with excitement. "I think you'll love the designs for the bathrooms." Standing, she tugged on his hand. "Let's go sit in my office. My computer is in there."

In her office, she nudged him toward the only chair in the room. "Sit. I'll get another chair from the kitchen."

"No need." Trent dropped into the office chair and then pulled Addie into his lap. "Okay, let's see what you came up with."

Trent kissed her neck as she pulled up the files, more than content to spend the entire evening doing just that.

"This is my plan for the wife's bathroom."

Trent looked over her shoulder at the computer screen. In the pictures, the claw foot tub remained as did the separate room for the toilet, but that was all that looked the same. In what had been an empty wall, she'd added two windows that cast light into a custom- built shower stall large enough for two. The old pedestal sink had been replaced with an extra long vanity that blended with the built-in makeup table making it look like one solid piece. Blue gray granite topped the vanity. Two additional mirrors hung over the long vanity in addition to the one already over the makeup table. Wall lights were positioned on either side of the mirrors. A chandelier hung from the ceiling and all new tiles lined the floor.

"It's gorgeous."

"Is there anything you'd change?"

He assumed since she'd come up with the design, she must like it and he planned on it being her personal space someday soon. "Not a thing. Let's see the other one."

OPENING HER EYES, Addie lifted her head and looked at Trent. His eyes remained closed, his breathing even. Careful not to wake him, she lowered her head back to his chest, a small sigh of contentment escaping her. Long before tonight she'd suspected that she loved him but kept the knowledge locked away, afraid that if she slipped it would send him running for the woods. Never in a million years had she expected him to blurt it out. While a part of her would've liked it to happen in a more romantic way, it didn't change the fact. Trent loved her. Joy bubbled up inside her. She'd already known he cared. Every one of his actions showed it. Love, though, she'd not anticipated, especially at this point in their relationship.

For a while she remained in bed cuddled up next to him, more content then she'd been in a long time. Outside she heard a car stop and a door slam. Not long afterward she heard a knock on her front door. With Trent looking so peaceful, she moved slowly, not wanting to wake him. Once free of his embrace, she grabbed her clothes from the floor. A quick peek out her bedroom window revealed a blue Ford she didn't recognize parked behind Trent's car.

Since Marcy Blake's visit no other reporters had stopped by, but Trent had warned her more would likely follow. With that thought in mind, Addie peeked out the peephole drilled into her front door. Then with a squeal of joy, she pulled open the door. "Oh, my God. I can't believe you're here," Addie half shouted, half cried when her brother, Rock, walked in. "Why didn't you tell me you were coming?" Tears of happiness coursed down her face as she hugged him.

Rock wrapped his arms around her. "I wanted to surprise everyone." He pulled back and kissed her cheek. "I stopped here first."

Unable to contain her surprise and happiness, she hugged him one more time and kissed him back. When she pulled away,

Rock's eyes scanned her hair and face. "Whose car is that in the driveway?"

Heat climbed up the back of her neck. She could just imagine what her hair looked like, and with a car in the driveway her brother knew she wasn't alone. "That's—" Addie began, but before she could finish, Trent appeared at the top of the stairs wearing nothing but his suit pants.

"Why didn't you wake me... " Trent's voice trailed off.

Embarrassment like she'd never known exploded inside her and her face burned as Trent came down the stairs half-naked as if he lived there.

"I guess I should've called first," Rock said from next to her. "I'm Rock, Addie's brother." Rock extended his hand when Trent stopped in front of him.

Addie watched Trent shake her brother's hand, still as cool as a cucumber. For a moment she wondered if he often greeted his girlfriend's family members like this. "Trent Sherbrooke," he said with no hint of embarrassment even though any idiot could figure out what they'd just been doing. "Your sister's boyfriend."

Rock held Trent's gaze and Addie held her breath. Her brother had hated her last boyfriend though she never knew why; they'd only met once. She didn't want that to be the case now. She might not see her brothers often, but they were an important part of her life. She valued their opinions. After a few seconds, Rock looked over at her again. "I saw pictures of you two together on the cover of some magazines at the PX. Not exactly the way a guy wants to learn about his sister's new boyfriend."

She could imagine how shocked she'd be if the tables were reversed. "Sorry. I meant to call you; I've just been busy."

Rock shot a look in Trent's direction then back at her. "I can see that," Rock said, always one to give her a hard time.

Another flame of heat burned her face. "Why don't you go in the kitchen? There are some leftovers from dinner. We'll be there in a minute."

Rock ruffled her hair. "If you want to get rid of me, just say so." He started down the hall. "Mind if I make some coffee?"

"Whatever," she called, happy her brother had complied. "I'm sorry, Trent. I didn't know he was coming."

"Don't worry about it. It gives me a chance to meet more of your family." He started to walk toward the kitchen, but before he got far, Addie grabbed his arm. "What's the matter?"

"Shouldn't you put a shirt on? This is my brother. He might know what we were doing, but I don't necessarily want to remind him."

"If it'll make you feel better." Trent walked back toward the stairs. "Should I put my tie back on, too?" he asked with humor.

Addie threw him a dirty look. "It's a good thing I love you because you're impossible." She heard Trent laugh as she continued on into the kitchen where her brother sat snacking away on the leftovers he found in the refrigerator while a pot of coffee brewed.

"So that's the famous Trent Sherbrooke," Rock said before Addie even sat down. "Looks like those magazine headlines were right. You and Trent Sherbrooke have been having fun together."

"Rock," she said, a clear warning in her voice. She didn't want her brother giving either of them a hard time tonight.

"What? I didn't say anything." He gave her a wide-eyed innocent look. "You two have been on the cover of magazines at least two or three times this week. And as long as you don't mind that and you're happy, then I am happy for you." He speared a piece of chicken with his fork.

"I don't love the media attention, but I am happy," she admitted. For the most part she tried to not think about the attention that went along with dating Trent. "Where are you staying while you're here?"

Her brother paused, his fork raised. "I was going to ask if I could stay here, but I get the impression you might not want me."

"Of course you can stay here."

Rock polished off the food on his plate and returned to the refrigerator for dessert, pausing at the coffee pot on his way back to the table. "I don't want to be in the way. I can stay with Mom and Dad."

The rich aroma of coffee had Addie following her brother's lead. "Mom will drive you crazy. Stay here."

"Addie, why don't you stay with me and let your brother have your place?" Trent said as he joined them in the kitchen, this time fully dressed including his shoes. "That way he has some privacy, and I have you. What do you think, Rock?"

Across from her, Rock studied Trent, neither man breaking eye contact. After what felt like a lifetime, her brother nodded and looked over at her. "I like the idea."

She didn't know what secret message had just passed between the two men and she didn't intend to find out either. In fact, she rather liked the idea, too. It would allow her not only to see Trent every day, but also fall asleep and wake up with him every day as well. "The place is yours. How long are you here for anyway?"

Rock swallowed the food in his mouth. "About two weeks." He raised his zeppola towards his mouth again. "Are you sure? Mom and Dad have the room."

"Positive. You'd go nuts there and it'll put me closer to my office."

The question of where her brother would stay settled, Addie stood. "I'm going to go pack. I'll be right back. Be nice while I'm gone, Rock." She jabbed her brother in the arm as she walked by him. "You too, Trent."

THIRTEEN

LATE FRIDAY NIGHT Addie unlocked Trent's apartment door. For almost a week now, she'd lived at his downtown apartment and everyday it became more and more natural to come back there after work. In fact, she didn't want to think about going back to living without him when her brother vacated her place.

Before walking any further in, she kicked off her sneakers. Tonight had been her final shift at the bakery. When she'd given her two-week notice, her mom had insisted it wasn't necessary. Despite her mom's claims otherwise, she'd promised that she'd work her scheduled hours that week. After much bickering back and forth, her mom conceded.

After depositing her shoes in a hall closet, she continued on into the well-lit but empty living room. Other than the lights there was no sign of Trent anywhere, which wasn't unusual. She learned he didn't leave his belongings around. Like her, he kept things neat and well ordered. His lack of presence in the living room meant he was more than likely in one of two places: his home gym or his office. Judging by the time, she guessed the office. He mentioned catching up on some extra work before the weekend.

"How's she feeling?" she heard Trent say as she approached the office, the door ajar. "Are you sure she'll be up for visitors this weekend?"

Addie stood in the open door as Trent spoke on his phone. With his back to the door, he'd yet to notice her. From his tone of voice and relaxed posture she assumed he spoke to a friend about a non-urgent matter. "Will Uncle Warren be there?"

Not a friend, a family member, maybe a sibling or one of his cousins. He had three brothers and a sister plus eight or nine cousins just on his father's side of the family, and they'd all at one time or another popped up in the media.

"That sucks, he must have been disappointed." Trent turned away from the windows toward the office door. The minute his eyes landed on her, he smiled and waved her in. "Listen I have to go, but we'll see you tomorrow. Congratulations again." Trent tossed his phone down as he strode toward her, closing the gap between them. Without so much as even a hello, he pulled her against him and kissed her as if ten months had passed since they'd last seen each other rather than ten hours. "I've missed you," he said when he pulled back, leaving her breathing ragged and her heart beating double time.

He slipped his hand under her T-shirt, his hands skimming up her rib cage as he kissed the pulse pounding in her neck. "I've thought about this all day," he whispered, his fingers undoing her bra.

Addie moaned when his hands took possession of her breast, his thumbs flicking back and forth across her nipples. "I missed you, too." She let her own hands slide up under his shirt and then up his back.

Trent pulled away from her neck, but his hands continued to tease. "That's it? You only missed me?" He sounded annoyed, but she knew it was only an act. "I couldn't think of anything but getting you naked and all you can say is you missed me? I guess I'll have to try harder from now on to pleasure you." With no other warning, he pulled her shirt over her head and tossed it over his shoulder.

"Okay, I really missed you."

"So that's how it's going to be tonight," he said with a wicked grin. Before she offered up any kind of answer, he unbuttoned her jeans and pulled them and her underwear down in one movement. Then he picked her up and deposited her on the edge of his desk. Spreading her legs wide, he stepped between them, his T-shirt rubbing against her nipples, which missed his earlier caress. "The next time we're apart I want you to think about tonight."

Without another word, he kissed her, his tongue sliding into her mouth as he drew her closer to him, his erection pressing against her. As he kissed her, his arms kept her locked against him. Then just like that he pulled away and switched his attention from her lips to her neck. As if he had all the time in the world, he worked his way down her body. When he took her left nipple in his mouth she sighed. When he switched to her other side and lavished that nipple with the same attention, she closed her eyes. Once he'd driven her a little mad, he began to pull away, but she dug her fingers into his hair in an effort to keep him there.

"Don't worry, I'll come back to here," he whispered and started trail of kisses downward.

"You better," she answered as he placed a kiss on the lower half of her rib cage.

Each kiss added to the explosive current that raced through her. At any minute Addie expected to explode into a million tiny pieces and die a happy woman. At least until his lips passed her navel and kept on moving south. In an instant some of the fog in her brain cleared and her eyes flew open. Addie placed her hands on either side of his head in a weak effort to stop him.

Trent looked up at her, but his hands remained on her thighs.

"Do you really want me to stop?" He trailed one hand up her thigh and over her, stopping just where his lips had been a moment ago. On cue Addie moaned as another level of desire took hold. Unable to do much more than shake her head no, she watched him smile before he returned his lips to the same spot his hand had been and kissed her.

Just when she reached the final breaking point, he pulled away. With swift movements, he tossed his own shirt in one direction and kicked his jeans to the side.

"I love you," he said as he slid inside, joining them together.

Her mind on overload, she could do little more than hold on for the ride as incredible pleasure and love flowed through her body.

"I MIGHT NEVER BE able to work in here again," Trent said a little while later. After their lovemaking on the edge of his desk, he'd carried her over to his chair and sat down with her on his lap. "You might need to turn one of those guest rooms into a new office for me because every time I come in here, I'll be distracted now."

"And whose fault is that?" she asked kissing his cheek.

Trent looked at her, one eyebrow raised. "I didn't hear you complaining a little while ago."

Addie ran a hand down his bare chest. "I'm not complaining now either, just making a statement."

"I'm glad you're home," he said, changing the topic of the conversation.

You're home; wow, she liked the sound of that. "Me, too. Who were you talking to when I walked in?"

Trent kept one arm locked around her waist while his other moved up and down her thigh. "Dylan. Callie had the baby yesterday morning."

With no further explanation she knew which cousin he referred to. Callie Talbot, previously Callie Taylor, had made all the headlines when the world learned her father was Warren Sherbrooke a few years earlier. The media had yet another field day when she married Warren's stepson Dylan Talbot, the current CEO of Sherbrooke Enterprises.

"I read somewhere she was due in October."

"The baby didn't get that memo," Trent joked. "I think Dylan said the baby was three weeks early."

"Did they have a boy or a girl?" She'd never met the couple, but it was a typical question.

"A boy. They named him James Warren Talbot. They invited us to their place in Connecticut for the weekend."

Addie ran the name through her head. "I like that name. It's has a nice ring to it." She guessed the middle name was in honor of Callie's father and wondered if James was another family name. "Us? Don't you mean you?"

"Nope. I don't want to go all weekend without you unless absolutely necessary."

Meeting the newest member of the family struck her as a close family affair. "Are you sure they won't mind?"

"Dylan specifically told me to invite you. He and Callie want to meet you. Besides, I want you to meet them, too. Dylan's a close friend. I've known him all my life. And you'll love Callie. Everyone does."

Addie rested her head on Trent's shoulder, tired from her long day. "Okay, when do we leave?"

The hand he'd used to caress her arm switched to her hair as he began to unbraid it. "In the morning after we get up. There's no rush. We'll come home Sunday night."

Closing her eyes, she smiled at his words. "I like when you say that."

"Say what?"

"We'll come home," she repeated as she cleared her head of all the day's activities and relaxed.

"Me, too." He paused, his hand stopping. "I've loved having you here this week." He began work on her braid again. "This place has felt like a home rather than just a place to sleep and shower since you've been here."

Content to listen to him speak, she remained silent, her eyes closed.

"Are you still awake?"

At his question she opened her eyes. "Yes, just comfortable."

"I don't want you to move back to your place when your brother leaves."

Attention caught, Addie sat up straight.

"I want you to move in here with me."

Much like when he'd told her he loved her, Trent's statement left her speechless. In all the years she'd read about him, she'd never read anything about him living with a woman. Of course that didn't mean he hadn't managed to keep such an arrangement under everyone's radar. "You want me to move in?" she asked just in case she'd misheard.

Trent nodded in response. "If you don't like it here we can move somewhere else. We don't have to stay in the city."

A unique mixture of apprehension and excitement gathered in her stomach. "No, it's not that. I love it here." She did love it, not only living in the city but Trent's apartment. "It's just we haven't been together that long."

"So what? I love you and want you with me. Time won't change that for me." A worried look passed over his face but disappeared before she could even blink. "Will it change anything for you?" The confident voice she'd come to know faltered.

"No, and if you're sure, I'd love to move in here with you. I'll have to rent my place or something, but that doesn't bother me."

At her response, Trent kissed her. A tender kiss filled with love rather than a hungry kiss like he'd greeted her with. "Good. Why don't we head to bed?" Before she could agree or protest, he stood with her in his arms and carried up to his room.

EVEN WITH HIS body sated and Addie next to him sound asleep, Trent remained awake. Fed up with staring at the ceiling, he climbed out of bed and pulled on pair of workout shorts. After a quick stop to grab a container of ice cream from the freezer, he parked his butt in front of the television. A quick scan through his movie collection brought up his favorite Mel Brooks movie, *History of the World Part I*, a ridiculous over-the-top comedy that required little brain power to follow along. More bored than hungry, Trent dug into the container of mint chocolate chip as the movie started.

By the time the movie hit the Spanish Inquisition segment, he'd finished the container of ice cream and realized he'd spaced out so much during the movie, he'd missed some of his favorite scenes. As the monks on the screen did their song and dance routine, he thought back to his meeting with Marty that morning. As planned, they'd met to discuss developments with his likely opponents. So far Daniel Potter still remained his main competition. Rumors that Harry Thatcher planned to run turned out to be just that, rumors. However, Marty received confirmation that Shelly Runnel intended to run as a Tea Party candidate for the seat in Washington.

His discussion with Marty about his competition wasn't what kept him awake now. Although pleased that Addie had quit the bakery, Marty had once again discussed their timetable. He wanted their relationship further solidified by the New Year at the latest.

The analytical part of him understood his advisor's position, but the human side of him rebelled every time Marty mentioned Addie's name. Sure, he'd gone into the relationship because Marty insisted she was his ticket into the Senate. Now though, he saw her as the woman he loved. The one he wanted to come home to every night and grow old with. Except in Marty's presence, he never considered the impact she may or may not have on his political career.

Ever since his meeting, when he'd agreed to consider a proposal before Christmas, his conscience had haunted him telling him to come clean with Addie about why he'd first asked her out. The devil in him insisted he keep his mouth shut. If she ever found out, who knew how she would react? And besides, what difference did it matter now? He loved her regardless of his original reasons. Which led him to another thought. If he loved her and planned to spend the rest of his life with her, why not just propose soon like Marty wanted? He intended to do it at some point anyway. She'd already agreed to move in with him. If he did it in, say, a month, it would get Marty off his ass and, if the advisor was correct, increase his chances in the election.

As the French King, played by Mel Brooks himself, interacted with the other characters on the screen, Trent's mind went back and forth. One minute positive they should stick to the original timetable they'd established for his relationship with Addie, and the next, prepared to hit the first open jewelry store he found and buy the biggest diamond engagement ring he could find.

"Trent?" Addie called from the doorway. "Are you okay?" Rubbing the sleep from her eyes, she shuffled into the room, her hair a mess from sleep and her old Suffolk University nightshirt ending just above her knees.

"Yeah, just wanted a little snack."

Addie looked at the empty ice cream container on the coffee table before sitting down next to him. As if programmed to do so, he placed an arm over her shoulders and pulled her into his side. "A little snack? I just picked that ice cream up yesterday."

"I guess I was hungrier than I thought. On our way home Sunday I'll buy you more." Mint chocolate chip was one of her favorites and a flavor he'd never had until she brought it home to help soothe her sore throat. "I'm ready to go back to bed now. You?"

She nodded. "I only got up to look for you."

———

SATURDAY HE DIDN'T CARE if he drew attention to them or not. So rather than take the more subdued Mercedes convertible he'd used since meeting Addie, he hit the road behind the wheel of his favorite new play toy, a Veyron Bugatti. He'd picked up the black Veyron with blood-red interior that spring, but as of late it had spent more time parked in the garage than on the road in an effort to make Addie more comfortable around him.

"Now this is more like what I expected you to drive," Addie said from the passenger seat as they sped down the highway. "Are you sure you want me drinking in here?"

Her statement brought to mind the comment she'd made about his car the first time he'd picked her up. "I am. Don't worry about it." He took a sip from his own travel mug. "So which do you like better? This or the Mercedes?"

"They're both okay," she answered, not sounding impressed with either.

Trent pulled his eyes away from the road long enough to shoot her a look. "Just okay? You don't say that a Veyron Bugatti is just okay. What kind of a car buff are you anyway?" One evening weeks earlier they'd had an in-depth conversation regarding sports cars through the years. She'd told him she'd learned all about them from her father and brothers, admitting she could not only change her own tire but also make various minor repairs to her own car if the need arose.

"Don't get me wrong. They're both great cars, but I'll take a 1957 Corvette convertible with the Ramjet Fuel Injection system first any day."

Trent looked over at her again. "Seriously? Cars today could do circles around that."

Addie lowered her travel mug. "Maybe, but it still managed zero to sixty in 5.7 seconds. Not to mention, it is gorgeous."

"And if you were to get one of those what color would it be?"

She didn't hesitate to answer. "Red, of course. It shouldn't be in any other color."

Trent laughed at her adamant reply. "They did make it in other colors, you know. Some people even liked them."

"They shouldn't have. Who ever thought that was a good idea must have been color blind."

He laughed again. "Okay, on that note let's talk about something else." He switched lanes when the car in front of them slowed down. "My family might bombard you with questions. They're not used to me bringing people to family gatherings like this. Just relax and enjoy yourself."

"I thought it was just going to be us and your cousin. I didn't know your whole family would be there." The lighthearted tone she'd used before disappeared.

"Not my whole family, but Dylan mentioned my cousin Jake and his wife are already there. My brother Derek and my cousin Courtney promised to stop in today, and my cousin Curt is coming tonight. My cousin Sara and her fiancée are flying in tomorrow, but we might not see them depending on when we leave. My father and stepmother visited yesterday and planned to leave this morning so we'll most likely miss them."

"Wow, that's a lot of people. For some reason I didn't think your family was that close."

"What made you think that?" The media printed a lot about the individuals in his family, but they never mentioned family squabbles.

From the corner of his eye he caught her shrug. "I don't know. It always seems like wealthy families are bickering amongst themselves, at least according to the magazines at the grocery store. I just assumed your family was the same way."

Since the only information she had to go on came from the media, he couldn't fault her. "My family isn't perfect, but we're tight. No matter what, we stick together. Don't worry, they'll love you."

"Maybe you better tell me a little more about your family before I meet them. The Cliff Notes version will do for now."

"Who would you like me to start with?"

Addie appeared to consider his question. "Maybe with your cousin, Courtney. I read a lot about your cousin Callie during the President's campaign, and Jake appeared in the media a lot before he married. I don't know much about Courtney."

It was true. Over the years he and Jake had kept the media buzzing enough that his cousin had managed to fly somewhat, although not completely, under the radar.

"Courtney is four years younger than me. Her mom is my father's sister, Marilyn. For the past year she has worked with my aunt at The Helping Hands Foundation, but I don't think she loves it there." Trent paused. What else might she like to know? "She has an older brother Scott and a younger sister Juliette. She spent a year and half living in Denmark and speaks Danish fluently. She's also fluent in Spanish and French."

"Wow. I know a little Italian, but I'm not even close to fluent."

"Courtney has always been great with languages. She picks them up quicker than anyone I know."

"Now what about your brother Derek? I know he is younger than you," Addie said.

During the rest of the two and half hour ride from Providence to Greenwich, Connecticut, Trent told Addie more about the individuals she'd meet that weekend, concluding with information about his brothers, Gray and Alec, and his sister, Allison, who wouldn't be there.

FOURTEEN

SINCE HIS COUSIN and her husband built the estate in Connecticut he'd visited just once. For the most part, Callie and Dylan still spent most of their time in New York City where the headquarters for Sherbrooke Enterprises was located. According to Dylan, however, they'd started to stay at the estate more and more as of late. While that meant more of a commute for him every day, Dylan said neither he nor Callie wanted the baby to grow up in the city. Trent could understand their sentiments. If and when he had children he wasn't sure he'd want them spending all their time in the city either. While the city, especially one like New York, provided a lot in terms of culture and activities, there was something nice about having acres and acres of land as your own personal playground. When the time came, he'd have to give the matter some serious consideration.

"Did they design this house themselves?" Addie asked as they waited for someone to open the front door.

They'd parked inside the large detached garage designed for visitors. From the moment they'd stepped from the car, he'd sensed Addie's designer's brain kick in. She'd paused to admire the interior and exterior of the garage as well as the flower gardens they passed as they followed the walkway to the house.

"Yes. Callie joked it took them longer to design it than it took for the actual construction. To some extent they based it on Dylan's father's estate in England."

A woman, perhaps his stepmother's age, dressed in black slacks and a white top, answered the door not long after they rang the bell. "Good morning, Mr. Sherbrooke," she said in a pleasant voice before smiling in Addie's direction. "Ms. Raimono, please come in."

The same woman had answered the door on his previous visit, but he had no idea of her name. His father and uncles would be disappointed in him. They all made it a point to remember the names of everyone that worked within the family homes.

"Please follow me. Mr. Talbot is in the back living room." The woman closed the door, then started down a hallway, her sensible black shoes silent on the gleaming floors.

"You weren't kidding when you said it was modeled after an English estate," Addie whispered into his ear as they walked. "I feel like I've just walked onto a PBS set."

Trent laughed. "I'll have to tell Dylan you said that."

Addie stopped and released his hand. "Don't you dare. He may take it the wrong way." Her glare, meant to reinforce her words, only made him laugh harder. "I mean it, Trent."

He took her face in his hands and kissed her forehead. "I promise, not a word. I was joking anyway."

"No you weren't. I know you better than that by now." She gave him a halfhearted smile. "I do love it in here. It's just not what I expected."

"You're right, I wasn't joking. But if it's that important I won't say a thing." He took her hand so they could catch up to the older woman again. "What did you expect?"

"Something more, I don't know, modern I guess is the right word. Maybe more along the lines of your apartment."

The woman in front of them turned down another hallway. "Their place in New York is more like my apartment. Dylan bought it before he met Callie. I think he likes it more than she does. I know they remodeled the apartment recently."

When they reached the large entryway, the woman who greeted them stopped just inside. "Mr. Sherbrooke and Ms. Raimono have arrived, Mr. Talbot. Does anyone require anything before I leave?"

Trent passed into the large room. Despite its size, it'd been laid out and furnished in such a way to give it a comfy and intimate atmosphere. Next to him, Addie's hand gripped his a smidge tighter.

"We're fine, Ester. Thank you. Enjoy your day off," Dylan answered. Seated in an arm chair, he had his long legs stretched out and a baby dressed in some kind of blue one-piece sleep outfit resting with his head on Dylan's chest. On the floor by his feet Lucky, Callie's dog, sat.

With a nod, Ester smiled. "Thank you, Mr. Talbot. Cora is in the kitchen if you require anything. I will see you tomorrow."

When Ester exited leaving the family alone, Trent crossed to his long-time friend, Addie's hand still attached to his. The last newborn he could recall seeing was his youngest brother Alec, and that had been a long time ago. He'd forgotten how tiny newborns were. "Congratulations, again." Trent extended his hand, his eyes still glued to the tiny infant. His brain found it difficult to process the sight of the baby on the chest of the once-confirmed bachelor. Yet, the now happily married husband and new father looked about ready to explode with pride.

Dylan shook with his right hand, his left never leaving the baby's back. "Thank you. I'm glad you could both make it." Dylan looked toward Addie. "It's nice to meet you, Addison. Please forgive me for not getting up." Always the proper English gentleman, Trent had never seen Dylan not stand to introduce himself to anyone. "My wife should be down soon."

Addie extended her hand in Dylan's direction. "Please call me Addie, and I understand. Your son is beautiful."

Although he doubted it possible, the pride and happiness on Dylan's face increased at Addie's words.

"Thank you. I would offer to let you hold him, but he just fell back asleep."

"Don't feel bad. I've barely gotten a glimpse of my nephew since I got here," Jake said from the sofa where he sat. "If he's not eating or getting a diaper change, he's attached to Dylan."

Not about to get in the middle of friendly family squabble today, Trent touched Addie's elbow and led her to the sofa. "Addie, my cousin Jake. And over there is my brother Derek." He nodded in his brother's direction as he sat. "Where are Charlie and Courtney?"

"Charlie went upstairs with Callie in case she needed any help getting in and out of the shower," Jake answered referring first to his wife. "Courtney went to answer a phone call from a friend."

"Allison called. She'll be here around six or so tonight," Derek added, referring to his twin sister. "Dylan's father decided to stay a few more days, too."

Trent had only met his friend's father once, the day Callie and Dylan married. The Viscount spent most of his time in England.

"I doubt you'd get him to admit it, but I don't think two days with his first grandson were enough," Jake added.

"Are you sure Callie's up for all these guests? Addie and I can head home and come back next weekend."

"Oh, no. You're not leaving before I get a chance to have a nice, long conversation with Addie, just like you and Charlie had at Cliff House. I'll need some time to share some embarrassing stories about you, and next weekend we have

Maureen's wedding to attend so I can't come back and do that."

Trent held back his reaction. He'd told his cousin's wife a few funny stories about Jake in private. He'd also shared a few more than embarrassing tales his cousin would've rather kept a secret. "You'll have to get her alone first and that's not happening."

Jake looked at Derek, who nodded, and then back at him. "Trust me, that won't be a problem. I have reinforcements."

Most times Jake's banter wouldn't faze him. His cousin was one of his closest friends and they'd grown up teasing each other. He also realized that he'd never tell Addie anything that would affect their relationship. Still, that didn't mean he wanted his girlfriend to know he'd slept with a bedroom lamp on until he was seven or that he'd had a favorite stuffed dinosaur named Rex that he'd slept with until his eighth birthday. His parents thought he'd thrown it away when he turned six, but he'd hidden it and just taken it out after going to bed. In fact, even after he'd stopped taking it to bed every night, he hadn't been able to part with it. Instead, he'd stashed it in his closet where it had stayed until he stumbled upon it when he was packing for his first year at Harvard.

"You have reinforcements for what?" Courtney Belmont, his cousin, asked as she entered the room and sat in an empty armchair.

"Our dear cousin was kind enough to share some of my embarrassing childhood memories with my wife," Jake answered. "I thought I'd repay the favor."

His younger cousin considered Jake's answer, then looked at him. "Don't worry, Trent. I have your back. I'll let Addie get to know you better before I let Jake expose her to all your secrets."

"Traitor," Jake teased.

"Now you have me intrigued. Maybe I should give you my

phone number, Jake. Then you could call me and share these stories with me," Addie said, joining the conversation.

Immediately, Jake pulled out his phone. "Great idea. What's your number?"

"Whose side are you on away?" Trent asked. While pleased that she felt comfortable enough to join in the conversation, he didn't relish the idea of her calling his cousin to discuss his secrets.

"In this case, your cousins," she answered and then proceeded to give Jake her phone number.

THE EASYGOING BANTER continued as they changed topics, and perhaps twenty minutes after they arrived Callie and Charlie joined them. Other than the small amount of weight she still carried from her pregnancy, his cousin looked great. In fact if not for the baby still asleep on Dylan's chest, he never would've guessed she'd given birth just a few days earlier. Next to her, Charlie looked as relaxed and friendly as the last time he'd met her.

"Have you and James been like that since we left?" Callie asked after she greeted Trent and Addie.

Dylan readjusted his outstretched legs before he answered. "I didn't want to wake him. Did you have any problems upstairs?"

"Of course not. I told you I would be fine. Charlie stayed in the bedroom and looked at a magazine while I showered. I didn't need any help."

"But you may have." Trent heard the concern in Dylan's voice and understood it. Although he'd never witnessed it, he knew childbirth was hard on a woman's body.

"Dylan, I'm okay. I had a baby not a heart transplant. Women do it all the time. I'm tired and sore, but not about to collapse on the floor. You need to relax a little." Callie placed her hand on her husband's shoulder and gave it a squeeze.

"She's right, Dylan. Callie's doing well," Charlie said. "But she does need to take it easy."

Trent watched in fascination as Callie scooped up her son, who'd just yawned and moved a tiny leg. "Would you like to hold him now that he's awake, Trent?"

"Wait a minute," Jake said, sounding put out. "Shouldn't his uncle get to hold him first? I saw him for five minutes yesterday before he started wailing to eat and Dylan's monopolized him all morning."

"I'd love to," Trent said with more passion than necessary just to annoy Jake. Then unable to resist the opportunity, he glanced around Addie toward his cousin. "Sounds like you're jealous. I think you need a son or daughter of your own."

Callie handed him the tiny bundle, showing him how to hold the baby and support his neck, then she stepped back. His initial gut reaction was to hand the baby back to her. In his large hands, James looked so small and fragile. Then the infant's little fist gripped his finger, the small gesture tugging at his heart. As he stared at the baby, he studied each perfect detail from the tiny fingers to the blue-gray eyes. And just like that he envisioned holding a baby of his own, one with Addie's chestnut brown hair and his dark blue eyes.

"I agree with Trent, Jake. James needs a cousin." Callie's voice shook him from his vision.

"And he'll have one in time for Sara's wedding."

Something similar to jealousy, perhaps envy, swept through him before happiness took its place. "Congratulations," he said before anyone else in the room responded.

"Why didn't you say anything sooner?" Callie hugged first her brother, and then her sister in-law. "When is the baby due?"

Both Jake and Charlie beamed with happiness. "April 4th. About two and half months before Sara's wedding," Jake answered.

The cousins would be less than a year apart, like him and

Jake. If Jake and Charlie had a son, Trent wondered if he and James would be as close as he and Jake had been.

"We've only told Mom and Dad so far. We thought we'd stop and tell Charlie's family this weekend, but Sean's out in California. Maureen and Ray are at a friend's retirement party in Portland and her sister has a sleepover with friends."

"I didn't know you had a sister."

"Half-sister," Charlie answered as his eyes went back to the baby in his arms. "She's twelve and I only met you this summer."

THE SUN WARMED her face as Addie leaned back on the stone bench. She and Trent had retreated outside to one of the well-manicured flower gardens. All around her pink and purple asters bloomed, as did some Russian sage with its blue flowers and silvery foliage. Sprinkled throughout the garden were Lemon Queen sunflowers, which bloomed in the late summer and early fall. Along the wall the gardeners had planted some yellow orange helenium, which if Trent hadn't told her differently she would've assumed were just plain old daisies.

"Do you know what is growing on the stone archway?" she asked. Thus far Trent had surprised her knowing several of the flowers and plants she didn't recognize.

"I think it's sweet autumn clematis, my mom had some in her garden, but I'm not positive." Trent spread his arms out along the back of the bench and stretched out his legs.

Her eyes roamed over the garden, amazed at all the variation and how well they blended together. "What about that one? Do you know what it is?" She pointed towards an electric-blue flower with five petals.

"Not a clue. You've exhausted my knowledge of plants."

Since they'd come outside he'd named at least ten or twelve different types of plants and shrubs.

Addie closed her eyes and enjoyed the soft breeze that blew around them. All too soon the temperatures in New England would start to drop and the snow would fall. "Oh, well. You still amazed me with how many you knew. You really learned all about them from your mom?" Trent didn't talk much about his mom, but he had shared that information.

"She adored flowers. In the summer she spent a ridiculous amount of time both in the gardens and in her greenhouse. Gray and I spent hours playing in the dirt while she planted and pruned her babies. I think she did more work than the gardeners my father paid. I guess I listened to her more than I thought when she talked about them."

She wanted to ask more about Donna Sherbrooke. Other than the fact she'd liked flowers and died years earlier, she knew nothing about the woman. Granted, a search on the Internet would have provided plenty of information, but she resisted doing that. She wanted to learn about the woman from Trent, yet she didn't want to pry if he found it too difficult to talk about her. Perhaps in time, he'd open up and tell her more.

"You're right, I do like your family." She opened her eyes again. "You guys sure like to give each other a hard time." She thought back to the conversation when they'd first arrived. While she'd been joking about Jake calling her to give up Trent's secrets, he'd immediately taken her number and then given her his. And while she was more than curious about Trent's past, she knew she'd never call Jake and ask.

"They loved you."

Much like all his answers since they'd come outside, his statement remained short. In fact, Trent had more or less only spoken when she asked him a direct question since lunch.

Addie turned so that she faced him, tucking on leg under her. "Are you okay?"

Trent looked at her. "Of course. Why?" He let his fingers brush against her shoulder.

"You've been quiet this afternoon."

"I have a lot on my mind, including a new resort up in Vermont." Trent fell silent again; the only sound was the rustling of leaves when the breeze blew. "You looked natural today holding James."

She had enjoyed holding the newborn. "I did a lot of babysitting for my neighbors. They didn't have any family in the area, so I'd often go babysit on Saturday nights so they could go out." Addie did the math in her head. "The oldest is fifteen now and her sister is almost twelve." Wow, time flew. "You looked comfortable yourself." The sight of Trent with the infant had turned her heart into mush.

"I liked it." Trent sounded surprised by the fact. "And it made me realize something."

Did she dare ask? "What?" she asked with hesitation.

"Someday I'd like a family of my own." The fingers on her shoulder stilled. "What about you?"

Sure she envisioned herself a mother at some point, but she'd never considered when. "A family would be nice."

"Large or small?" he asked. "We both come from big families, and maybe you disagree, but I liked growing up with a lot of siblings. Yeah, they drove me nuts, hell, they still do, but there was always someone around. Callie was an only child growing up. She told me she always dreamed of a brother or sister."

Addie could relate to Trent's comments. Her brothers drove her insane, but she wouldn't trade them for anything in the world. "My cousin Chloe is an only child. I think that's why she spent so much time at my house growing up. I'd want at least two children."

"Two." He considered her response. "I was thinking more like three or four, but if you want two I'd be happy with that."

Addie said a silent thank you that her butt was already

planted on the bench because if she'd been standing she'd be flat on her behind at the moment. "I thought you were talking in general terms," she said when her brain began sending messages to her mouth again.

Trent sat up straight and looked at her. "I'm not saying we should get started now, but that's how I see you. Where I want us to be someday."

"Me, too," Addie said around the lump in her throat. He hadn't proposed or anything, but he'd made his intentions crystal clear.

The serious expression on his face faded. "Of course if you want to practice, I'm all for it. We could head upstairs right now."

"You're impossible," she said tickling his side.

"What? It's not like anyone would notice."

She tickled him again. "We can start practicing all we want when we get home tomorrow. Believe it or not I'd like to spend more time with your family."

FIFTEEN

"ARE you sure you don't want to come?" Trent asked as he added another undershirt to his suitcase.

"Positive. I'll use the time to get some extra work done. Besides, you'll only be away two nights. We'll both survive." Three weeks had passed since their weekend in Connecticut and in that time they'd not spent a night apart.

After adding some underwear and socks to the bag, he zipped it up. "If you say so."

"Just think how happy I'll be to see you when you get back." The security panel near the bedroom door beeped and Addie hopped off the bed to answer it. "I bet that's Chloe. She'd said she'd stop by." Pushing the answer button on the panel, she greeted the doorman downstairs. As she suspected, her cousin had arrived. "Please send her up."

"Now I get it. While I'm gone you two are going to party," Trent said, his lips turned downward in a frown as he took her into his arms.

She pasted on her best guilty look. "You guessed it. While you're up in Vermont, we're going to prowl the city for men."

Trent's eyes grew wide. "I thought you just had a big house

party planned. But if that's the case you're definitely coming with me." They both knew full well she had eyes only for him. "I might even handcuff you to my side."

"If anyone should be worried, it's me," Addie said. "With all those beautiful, rich women running around." The purpose of Trent's trip was to meet with the managers of an exclusive ski resort and spa that Sherbrooke Enterprises had just acquired. The resort, located on Stratton Mountain, had been visited by big name celebrities and an heiress. From the little she'd read about it, the resort wasn't the type of place you took the family for a ski trip unless your yearly income included seven figures or more.

Trent's expression became serious, his eyebrows coming together and he gripped her shoulders. "You have nothing to worry about. I love you." From the hallway the doorbell rang, but he kept his hands on her shoulders. "Addison."

"I was teasing, Trent. I'm not worried." She didn't lie. Thus far he'd given her no reason not to trust him and believe that he loved her. "And I love you." The bell rang again. "Come on, let's go downstairs."

Before he released her, he kissed her. "Go ahead. I'll be right down."

Chloe looked poised to ring the bell again when Addie pulled open the door. Still dressed in the clothes she'd worn to the bakery, she had a large canvas bag slung over one shoulder and held a pastry box in her hands. "You did say to come over after work, right?" She followed Addie into the living room. "I can come by tomorrow otherwise."

"I was upstairs helping Trent pack." She accepted the box and turned, intent on going to the kitchen.

"Actually, I brought those for Trent," Chloe said before Addie moved another inch.

"Brought what for me?" Trent entered the room, his leather jacket on and his suitcase in hand.

"Uh, some cannoli. Addie told me how much you like them."
She toyed with her gold hoop earring as she spoke.

Trent didn't hesitate. He moved in and removed the pastry
box from Addie's hands. "Fantastic. These babies are coming
with me." He dropped his suitcase and opened the box. "I don't
know if these will last the whole ride up." He looked in
Chloe's direction. "Thank you, Chloe," he said before he
turned back to Addison. "I need to go. I'll call you tonight." He
kissed her as if her cousin didn't stand just feet away. "I love
you."

Despite all the kisses they'd shared, he still somehow
managed to take her breath away. "Love you, too. Have a safe
trip." She watched him leave before collapsing into a chair. It
was going to be a long two nights.

"Oh, my god! How do you live with him and get anything
done?" Chloe said, her voice animated and full of excitement.
"I'd sit around here all the time and just look at him."

Addie laughed and tossed a pillow at her cousin. "You're
nuts, you know that."

In return Chloe tossed the pillow back, aiming for Addie's
head, but she ducked and it sailed right over the chair. "It's true.
The guy is crazy hot."

Rather than admit she did find herself just staring at him
from time to time, she jumped to her feet. "How about a tour
before we look at those paint samples you brought?"

Ready for a place of her own, Chloe decided to move out of
the apartment she shared with two roommates and rent Addie's
place with the plan to buy at some point.

"Please. I've been dying to see this place."

Like a perfect host, Addie gave her cousin the grand tour of
the two-floor penthouse. In each room Chloe gushed over something whether it be the furniture or the view. It reminded Addie
of her internal thoughts the first time she walked in. Even now, a
few months since her first visit, the place overwhelmed her

sometimes. On more than one occasion she'd come home and stared, amazed that she now lived here.

"This place is incredible," Chloe gushed as she retrieved her bag with the paint samples. "I bet you're not mad that I sent that picture into the paper now."

Chloe's words drifted into the kitchen where Addie stood getting drinks from the refrigerator. *Maybe I misheard. Maybe she said, "you're not mad about the picture."* "What did you say?" She gripped the two bottles of flavored water, the plastic cold against her skin.

"That you're not mad about the picture in the *Gazette*." She placed the canvas bag with the paint cans and the unpainted wood blocks on the table. "You were furious when it came out." Chloe began to spread newspaper on the kitchen table. "At first I thought maybe I'd made a mistake sending in the picture."

Addie slammed the water bottles down onto the table. "You sent that in?" In the blink of an eye, her shock changed into anger. "Why would you do that?"

Her cousin looked down at the table and cleared her throat. "It seemed like a good idea at the time. I thought maybe it would help your business." She raised her head and met Addie's eyes, but her fingers fiddled with the edges of the newspaper. "I thought you'd figure it out after awhile."

The last person she'd ever even consider was Chloe. There had been several customers in the bakery that day and she'd assumed it had been one of them. "I can't believe you did that, Chloe. You should've told me sooner. For weeks it drove me nuts. Trent even had his campaign advisor look into it."

Shit, Trent. She'd have to tell him. How would he react? The picture itself hadn't upset him much. At least it appeared that way then, but Chloe had violated his privacy, too.

"Come on, Addie. Please don't be mad at me. Your business did improve, so did all the bakeries. Nothing bad happened." Chloe pleaded in the same manner she had when they had been children and she'd done something wrong. "And it's just a picture of you two drinking coffee."

She fought down her anger. The picture wasn't the issue. If her cousin had taken it and then just sent it to her she wouldn't have cared. But that wasn't the case. She'd gone behind her back and shared it with the world. Okay, maybe not the world, but the whole state. "I... you," she struggled for the right words. "You had no right, Chloe. You never should have sent it." She placed both hands on the table. In time she'd forgive her cousin, but right now she needed her to leave. "I can't do this now, Chloe. Some other time maybe. I'd rather if you left for now."

"Come on, Addie. It was just one picture. Besides, now look at the two of you. You're living together and he loves you. Heck, I saw a picture of you on the cover of *The Star Report* leaving a Starbucks in Connecticut together."

Addie began to fold up the newspaper when her cousin made no move to clean up. With her patience gone, she snapped at Chloe. "That's different. My own cousin didn't take that picture and send it in."

Chloe snatched the newspaper from Addie's hands. "Fine, be that way. Call me when you get over it." After stuffing the paper back in her bag, Chloe spun on her heel and marched out.

STILL IN THE kitchen long after her cousin left, Addie took another long sip from her flavored water. Every time she thought about what her cousin did, the urge to scream overwhelmed her. Everything her cousin said was true. No harm had been done. Regardless, Chloe had been way out of line. She'd made the situation even worse by not coming clean when Addie first admitted how much it bothered her.

Family. Maybe the makers of dictionaries should change the definition of the word. A more appropriate description than the one in current dictionaries would be "group of people whose sole purpose is to drive you crazy."

Addie eyed the wine refrigerator built into the kitchen. Something a little stronger than water sounded like a good idea. If she had just one now, she'd relax a little and still be able to get some work done. Later before Trent called and she told him about Chloe, she'd have another one or two.

In the end she'd worried over nothing. When she told him about Chloe's confession, he hadn't raised his voice or shown any evidence that he cared who sent the picture in. He had used a few choice words in terms of what he thought of Chloe and her behavior toward Addie. Before then she'd never heard Trent swear like that, but during their conversation he'd sounded like her brothers when they got into heated arguments with each other and they knew their mother wasn't around to hear.

Perhaps thanks to the way Trent handled the news, she climbed into their bed an hour after their phone conversation more at ease. Anger toward Chloe remained, but at least her worry about Trent's reaction no longer ate away at her. Even so, she remained awake a long time tossing and turning. Without Trent's six-foot-plus tall frame filling his side of the bed and his arms wrapped around her, the king size bed felt more like an empty abyss rather than a warm comfortable sanctuary. Sometime well after midnight Addie drifted off into a restless slumber.

ADDIE HIT print and then opened another file on her computer. That morning she'd woken up early and arrived at her office before seven o'clock. She'd worked straight through until lunchtime when a florist arrived with a large arrangement of flowers and a card from Trent that read "Thinking of you. See you tomorrow. Love Trent."

The first time she'd ever received flowers at work, she placed them right next to her computer so she could see them as she worked. Addie remained in front of her computer until four when she'd left with one thing on her mind, a nap. Whether because of her poor night's sleep or early morning, she feared she'd fall asleep right there at her desk. More grateful than ever for her short commute now, she'd gone back to their apartment and straight to bed not even bothering to change out of her work clothes.

Now though, after a two-hour nap and a snack, her brain could function again. So dressed in one of Trent's T-shirts and some sweatpants, she sat in his home office finishing a proposal. When she'd first moved in, he offered to convert one of the two guest bedrooms into an office of her own. After she'd declined, he'd insisted she use his whenever she wanted. According to him, he didn't use it much anyway. He preferred to do most of his work at Sherbrooke Enterprises and only brought stuff home when he had no other choice.

From the credenza behind her, the printer stopped. A quick peek at the device revealed it needed paper, an easy fix, assuming she could find some. If it were her office she'd keep reams of paper close to the printer itself. Since the credenza had no drawers, only shelves lined with books, she'd need to look elsewhere.

When a thorough search of the tall three-drawer file cabinet near the printer turned up nothing, she glanced around the room. "Where would he keep paper?" The bookshelves on the far wall contained only books and a few binders. Other than the closet, the only place she hadn't checked was the desk. She pulled open the top middle drawer. As expected it contained only pens and a box of business cards. The extra deep drawer on the left contained more hanging files. "Please have some paper." She tugged open the top right-hand side drawer. Once again out of luck. She started to close the drawer when she caught a glimpse of the picture Chloe sent in.

Addie picked it up and unfolded it. Even though Chloe had taken the photo with her camera phone it was a good picture. Now that she examined it in more detail, she realized she should've suspected someone that worked at the bakery took it. She could see the front windows and door, which faced the street in the picture. Only a person near or behind the counter could have snapped the picture from that angle. She read the headline above the picture. The whole day seemed liked a lifetime ago.

Prepared to put it back, she folded it up. Before she dropped the paper inside what had been underneath it caught her eye, a neat spiral bound binder with the name Miranda Bergman typed under a picture. More curious than anything, she picked it up and found a similar one under it with the name Vanessa Mitchell under a photo. Without a second thought, she picked that one up as well as a third and final one with the name Serena Tasca on the cover. As she held the final slim binder, a manila file folder, which had been stuck to the bottom of it, fell onto the desk. When she saw the name Addison Raimono hand printed in bold black letters on the side tab, she stopped breathing.

Sitting down, she pushed the other binders off to the side and opened the folder with her name on it. Her hand shook as she read the top page, which listed her basic personal information such as her birthday and address. Unable to stop herself, she turned the page and read more. Each page she read added to the file's mysterious purpose. It contained everything from where she'd been born and gone to school, to when her family had first immigrated to the United States from Italy in the early 1900s. There were pages documenting her work history, her driving record and even her credit score.

When she reached the end of the file she closed it. When had he gotten such information and why would he want it? Had he done a background check on her when they first started dating to make sure he could trust her? To make sure she wasn't someone out to use him for his money? Wealthy people signed prenups for that reason. Maybe he'd thought to protect himself long before they approached that stage. Was that what those other binders were about as well? Had he dated those women too in the past?

Should she read those? Addie chewed on her nail and eyed the stack. They might contain the same kind of personal information her file did. "They're none of my business," she said even as she picked up the top one and studied the cover. A picture of an attractive twenty-something-year-old woman with dark brown hair occupied the corner space, the name Serena Tasca underneath. Neither the name nor the face rang any bells, but the picture on another one did. Miranda Bergman, a woman close to Addie's age, had begun to hit media headlines when Addie had been in high school. The sole heiress to an international restaurant chain, her father also owned a professional sports team, and for a short time she'd been engaged to a wealthy Greek businessman's son. With slow movements, she opened the binder. The first page was similar to the one in her file. It contained Miranda's birthday, parent's name, and several address around the country. The binder also went on to list Miranda's educational background and hobbies. Unlike her own, Miranda's credit score and driving record were not mentioned. Instead, her estimated net worth glared back at her. What surprised Addie more than anything else in the report was the benefit analysis near the end. She'd never seen anything quite like it and the more she read it, the less it made sense.

Curious if the other two binders contained a similar analysis, she reached for Serena's file again. This one too contained a boatload of information as well as the same bizarre analysis. Addie skipped the third one altogether. Even without looking she knew what she'd find. Her hands shaking, she stacked everything back up only then noticing the date in the bottom right hand corner of the cover page, July 8 one week after he bumped into her outside the bakery. In fact all three had the same date, killing her idea that these were all women Trent had dated in the past.

Did the pages in her folder have a date on them? She grabbed her own folder back. Sure enough, the cover page was dated one day after her and Trent's picture showed up in the paper. The blueberry muffin she had after her nap rolled in her stomach, and she thought she might be sick.

There had to be a reasonable explanation for all this. There just had to be. Addie took in a deep breath, exhaled and repeated a few more times until the queasiness in her stomach went away. Think. What purpose could he have for this information? Determined to come up with something, she propped her chin up in her hands. As the seconds ticked by nothing came to mind that could explain what she'd stumbled upon. Her only option was to ask him.

Talk about a great conversation opener. "Hey, Trent, why do you keep personal dossiers of women in your desk?" Not only that, what if she didn't like the answer? This wasn't just some client she worked for. She loved him and he loved her. Or did he? For the first time since he'd said the words, she doubted him.

Knock it off. Hear what he has to say first. She repeated the sentiment at the same time her phone rang, Trent's ring tone filling up the room. After a moment's hesitation she answered it.

"Are you home yet?" he asked after they exchanged greetings.

"I left work early. Right now I'm just doing some work in your office." She looked at the files before her, the women on each cover starring up at her.

"Are you okay? You're not getting sick again are you?" His voice took on concern.

Not anymore. "No, I'm fine. Just tired. I didn't sleep well last night." Weeks earlier she'd had strep and it had drained her.

"Me either. I missed you next to me," Trent answered. "Did you get the flowers I sent?"

"They're beautiful. I left them on my desk." Should she question him now? She wanted answers more than anything, but a face-to-face conversation might be better. "When do you think you'll get home tomorrow?" With any luck he'd get back early.

"If everything goes as planned, by nine."

She stifled a groan. Of all the nights for him to get home on the late side. "Do you expect any problems?" Unable to look at the women's faces any longer, she stuffed the binders back into the drawer.

"No, but you never know. Then there's traffic. If you have plans or want to work late go ahead. I'll text you when I'm half an hour from home."

"Okay, sounds good. I do have a lot of work." She heard the uncertainty in her voice. How she wanted to question him now. She didn't know how she'd ever make it through the whole day tomorrow without knowing the truth.

"Get as much done as you can. I don't want anything distracting you when I get back." Unlike most times, his sexy voice didn't set her pulse racing.

Addie focused on making her voice sound as normal as possible. "Will do. I'll see you tomorrow. Love you."

"Love you too, sweetheart. Get a good night sleep."

She hung up the phone knowing one thing: she'd not be getting a good night's sleep tonight.

SIXTEEN

THE LIVING ROOM looked perfect and the music in the background added the final romantic touch. Now he just needed to arrange the food for dinner. Addie would be home any minute. As promised, he'd sent a text telling her he'd be home in thirty minutes, but while she'd believed he'd been in the car when he sent the message, he'd been home arranging the living room for a romantic dinner. Tall, white taper candles flanked a flower arrangement on the round kitchen table he'd moved into the living room. While he'd considered using the dining room, he wanted the table he set to be intimate. The overhead lights were dimmed as low as possible. Additional candles flickered around the room adding to the atmosphere. An open bottle of wine stood ready near his wine glass. All in all, he'd done a good job in his opinion. Addie or perhaps his sister would've done even better, but this was his first attempt. In the past when he'd wanted a romantic setting for dinner, he'd pick up the phone and make a reservation. Tonight, though, he didn't want an audience, just his Addie. The two nights he'd gone without her had been two of the longest he'd ever experienced.

Back in the kitchen, he opened the first takeout container

from Lucerne. Although the restaurant didn't offer takeout service, they'd agreed to prepare meals for him. They'd even had one of their employees deliver it. A young man perhaps seventeen or eighteen who most likely bused tables had arrived right on time and Trent had given him a generous tip.

Thinking about all the meals he'd eaten there, Trent tried to arrange the plates of the food the way they did. When the containers were empty, he eyed the plates. They were close but not quite as nice as when the restaurant served them. For tonight they'd have to do. Using the plate covers provided by the restaurant, he covered the food as the front door opened.

"What's all this?" Addie's voice reached him.

Right on time. "A surprise." He walked over and greeted her with a kiss. "For our anniversary."

"Anniversary? What are you talking about?" Addie eyed him as if he'd lost his mind while away. "If you mean of our first date that's not today."

Trent slipped his fingers under shoulder bag and slipped it off her arm. Then he took her hand and led her to the table. "Four months ago today, I bumped into you outside the bakery." How that one day had changed his life. "If not for that accident, I wouldn't have met you." He pulled out a chair and gestured for her to sit. "Don't move; I'll be right back." Addie nodded but rather than smile at him, she frowned.

When he returned with the prepared plates, she remained where he'd left her, the frown as well as another emotion he couldn't label on her face.

"You cooked this?" she asked with amazement when he pulled off the plate cover.

"No. The fabulous chefs at Lucerne did. I just put it on the plates." While he could cook simple things like pasta and eggs, anything more elaborate was out of the question. Reaching for the wine, he poured some in her glass and then his. "Are you okay? You look tired." Dark purple smudges were under her eyes and her face looked pale.

"I didn't sleep well with you gone." She picked up her fork, the frown changing to a tight smile. "I'm glad you're home."

Conversation over dinner remained minimal and Trent assumed her lack of sleep was to blame. He hadn't slept well either, but right now weariness didn't bother him. In fact, he suffered from just the opposite. His insides were vibrating and he suspected he could run the Boston Marathon and set a new course record.

"Sit there and I'll get dessert." He removed her plate when she said she was done. Although she'd claimed the food tasted delicious, she'd eaten less than half while he'd cleaned his plate.

Like dinner, he'd ordered the same dessert she'd ordered the night they'd dined there.

"You didn't need to do all this," Addie said when he put down the dessert.

The music in the background changed as the romantic ballad by a female singer he didn't recognize changed and a male belted out a classic rock ballad. "Yes, I did," he said. Unable to wait until after dessert as he'd planned, Trent cleared his throat and reached for her hand across the table. "I wanted tonight to be special. A night you'd remember forty years from now." His mouth grew dry and he paused in his speech for a drink.

Addie didn't move or say a word as she watched him but her mouth curved downward, her frown from before back in place.

"Before you, I didn't think love was in the cards for me. I knew it existed, but I'd never experienced it. Now, I can't imagine my life without you." He pulled out the diamond and platinum ring he'd hidden under a flower petal. "Addison Raimono, will you marry me?" He slipped the ring onto her left hand.

Addie's eyes looked at the ring, then back up at him, but

rather than smile or cry out with joy she pressed her lips together and swallowed.

"Addie, this is where you're supposed to say yes." He tried to joke, but a sinking sensation set into his stomach.

"Trent, I love you and there's nothing I'd like more than to marry you." She said the words he wanted but her tone made his stomach sink further. "But I need to ask you something before I accept this ring."

"Ask me anything." He had no secrets to hide from her.

"Do you promise to answer honestly?"

Trent nodded, prepared for a question about his past.

Addie took a deep breath. "The other night I did some work in your office. The printer ran out of paper so I looked for more. I found something strange in your desk."

He kept only work related stuff in there. "Okay, what?"

Without answering, she left the table and came back from his office with something in her hand. "These." She placed several binders and a folder on the table near his dessert. "What are they?"

He'd forgotten about the binders from Marty. After the meeting when Marty gave them to him, he'd tossed them in his desk and not looked at them again. What he should've done was put them through the paper shredder. He stared at them, willing an answer to come that wouldn't make him look like a complete ass.

"I read them all. I know I shouldn't have, but I did. Why did you need all that information about me and those other women?"

He stared at the materials. His mind a blank slate.

"At first I thought maybe these women were people you dated before me. That maybe you checked out all your girl-friends, afraid they were after your money or something." He heard the catch in her voice. When he looked up he saw the suspicion on her face. "But they all have a July date on them, including mine."

Complete honesty was his only option now. "You know that I have a less than stellar reputation." He'd have to start at the beginning.

Addie nodded, clasping her hands in front of her.

"My campaign advisor was concerned it would hurt my chances at election. His solution—find a wife long before the election." Just talking about the plan made him feel like a jerk. "He had connections with some high-profile families who would be interested in a marriage of convenience. These three women come from those families."

"That's insane but whatever. That explains those binders. But what about my information, and shouldn't you be here right now with one of those women instead of me?" she asked glaring at him.

"I agreed with his marriage of convenience proposal since everyone involved would be on the same page." Did he have to tell her everything? Could he just tell her he'd changed his mind after meeting her? If he did that he could use her previous assumptions about her file.

"Trent, are you going to answer me?" she asked when he remained silent too long.

No, she needed the whole truth. Any lies might come back and haunt him later. "After that picture showed up in the paper, Marty checked into you and you reminded him of my cousin Callie and Jake's wife, Charlie. America loves both of them. He decided that you were the perfect woman for me." Trent avoided Marty's exact words that day.

"And you agreed?"

"Yes and no. I tried to convince him otherwise at first. When he wouldn't budge I told him I would consider it but made no promises."

Addie's eyes became glossy. "Why?"

"Those other women knew what they were getting into with me. They understood we'd only date and marry because I needed a wife, not because I loved them. You wouldn't have known any of that."

"So you never would've asked me on that first date if Chloe hadn't sent in that picture and caught Marty's attention." She wiped a tear from her cheek.

"I don't—"

"Be honest for once, Trent. Would you have asked me out?" she asked in a harsh raw voice.

He hung his head, unable to meet her eyes. "No. I would've picked one of those women and after you finished decorating my office, we probably never would've seen each other again." He didn't want to see her reaction, but he had to make things right so he looked up.

She'd clenched her jaw tight and tears streamed down her cheeks. "So all of this," she gestured around with her hand. "Our time together and this proposal are part of a plan to fix your reputation." Her voice broke but she didn't look away.

Her words and reaction chilled him to the bone. A tense silence enveloped the room as he searched for the right words. When he settled on his words, he reached for her hand, but she pulled it away crossing her arms over her chest.

"When I first asked you out, it was because of Marty's plan." Cold sweat trickled down his back as he started. "But almost right away, I forgot all about it. When we were together, it was because I wanted to be with you, not because I needed a wife." Addie's expression remained the same. "The day I told you I love you, I meant it. Addie, I love you and want to marry you because of you, not Marty or some half-ass plan." Panic rose inside him.

"No. When I said I love you, I meant it. You've just been using me for your own goals," she said, bitterness lacing her every word.

Afraid of where the conversation was headed, he stood and walked around the table. Taking her by the shoulders, he turned her toward him. "That's not true. Every word I've said, I have meant. Addie, I love you."

She sniffled and wiped another tear away. "I don't know if I can believe you." She slipped the ring off her finger. "I know I cannot accept this." The ring hit the table as his heart hit the floor. "I do love you, Trent, but I need to go."

"Don't leave like this." Tears gathered in his eyes, and he gripped her shoulders tighter.

"Please, let me go."

Other than physically keeping her there by force, he couldn't think of any way to make her stay. "Not until you promise to think things through. Consider giving me another chance." He'd envisioned this night so much differently. Right now they should be wrapped up in each other's arms, talking about wedding dates.

Addie took hold of his wrists and pulled at them. "I can't make any promises." She stood when he released her shoulders. "I'll get my stuff some other time." She went toward the door without looking at him again.

He couldn't move his feet; they were cemented in place. "Where are you going?"

She continued walking, answering him as she went. "My house or I guess Chloe's house."

He watched in silence as the door opened and closed, sending a single teardrop down his cheek.

SHE MADE it into her car before the dam broke and tears poured down her face. How could it have all been fake? She'd been confident that his feelings matched her own. And what kind of a person manipulated another like he had?

Addie dropped her head against the steering wheel, sobs racking her entire body. She'd been sure that he was the one despite the differences between them. Never in her wildest imagination had she expected their relationship was a ruse, a plan to fix his reputation.

For quite a while she gave her emotions free reign. Then when her head began to pound she sat up. Ignoring the burning in her eyes, she took several deep gulps of air and wiped the tears with the sleeve of her sweater. Confident she'd make it home in one piece, she started the car and headed for Chloe's.

When Chloe opened the door, she took one look at her cousin and hugged her. Neither remembered that just days earlier they'd argued. Instead, Chloe led her into the kitchen, dropped a full container of mint chocolate chip ice cream in front of her and waited.

Addie's first instinct was to tell her cousin everything, but she held back. How much should she share? She loved Chloe much like a sister. However, now she wondered if she could trust her with the whole truth. She'd didn't fear she'd leak the story the way she had the picture. Chloe wasn't cruel, but what if she said something to a friend? Who knew what her friends would do with the information?

"Do you want to talk?" Chloe asked, well into her own ice cream container. "If not, that is okay."

The cold ice cream soothed her achy throat brought on by all her sobbing. "We had a big fight. Do you mind if I stay here for awhile?"

Chloe gave her a hug. "Of course. Technically, this is still your house," she reminded her. "And if you need me later, I'm here."

Addie nodded, then dug in for more ice cream.

———

THE METAL FRAME of the futon dug into her back causing even more discomfort when she woke the next morning. Even though her cousin had offered her the use of her old bedroom,

Addie declined and slept on the futon she'd left in the spare bedroom. She'd always intended to replace it with a proper bed. Since until recently she'd never had any guests the entire two years she lived here, she never had.

This morning, as the metal bars poked into her back, she wished she'd invested in that extra bed. Rubbing at her temples she closed her eyes again, the sunlight making her headache worse. The last time she'd had a headache this bad was the one time she'd tried giving up all caffeinated beverages. She'd lasted only two days before she grabbed a jumbo iced tea from a nearby fast food restaurant.

Addie groaned as her stomach rolled, and for a moment she feared the ice cream from the night before would make a repeat performance. *That's what I get for eating a whole container of ice cream.* She swallowed down the bile rising in her throat. *Never again.*

A soft knock sounded on the door, followed by Chloe's voice. "I'm leaving for work. I left some bacon and waffles on the counter for you. Will you be here when I get home?"

"I will," Addie answered. "Possibly in the very same spot if this headache doesn't go away."

The door opened and Chloe poked her head inside. "There is some extra strength Excedrin in the bathroom. See you later."

Addie waited until she could lift her head without the pounding making her dizzy. Still in the pj's she'd borrowed from Chloe, she went downstairs. Perhaps a coffee would send the drummer in her head on his way.

The combined smell of bacon and waffles hit her head-on when she entered the kitchen. Her stomach, still upset from the previous night's overindulgence, flipped sending Addie on a mad dash to the bathroom, which she made it to just in time.

Once confident her stomach held nothing else, she splashed cold water on her face. Vomiting was the least pleasant physical response in the world and something she rarely did. Patting her face dry, she looked into the mirror. While her tan from the summer had faded, she usually had more color than she did now. Making her appearance even worse were the purple smudges under her bloodshot eyes. Man, was it a good thing today was Saturday. She looked like hell. Had she looked this bad last night, too? If so, no wonder Chloe appeared worried when she opened the door.

There's nothing you can do about it now. Addie turned off the light. Besides, she had other problems, all of them with the name Trent attached to them. How could he treat her this way? Sure, she'd read that he was a carefree playboy, but she'd never heard him called cruel. The way he'd manipulated their relationship bordered on cruelty in her mind. And if what he said was true and he did love her, how could she ever know for sure? Could she ever hear him say those words and not wonder if he had his reputation and political career in mind?

Addie skipped the bacon and waffles and made herself a hot cup of herbal tea. As much as she wanted a nice big hot coffee, she knew her stomach would never handle it. Addie washed some headache medicine down with her tea. Man, she hoped Trent had as crummy of a night as she had. When she walked out, she'd noticed the distraught expression on his face. "He was probably upset his plan backfired," she muttered to herself as she grabbed her toast from the toaster.

Something soft and fuzzy rubbed against her leg and Addie slammed her knee into the table when she jerked it away. "Ouch." Glancing under the table she spotted Hugh, her cousin's black cat. A stray rescued from a local animal shelter, Hugh's entire body was black except for one small patch of white around the eye. Not your typical cat, at least in terms of the ones she met before, Hugh loved human companionship much the way a dog did. "I forgot you were here." She scratched the cat behind the ears. Hugh purred, then licked her hand before curling up into a ball on her feet.

Both Addie and the cat stayed in the kitchen. Addie sipping her tea and thinking about Trent, while Hugh kept her bare feet warm. "This isn't solving anything, Hugh." While she couldn't solve her problems with Trent, she could solve one of her other problems, her lack of clothes. All of her stuff remained at his place. While at some point she'd have to get it, she wasn't up for that today. Thankfully, she had a credit card and a nearby mall. After depositing her half-eaten dry toast in the trash, she headed upstairs.

HE'D TRIED CALLING her five times while she shopped. When the fifth one came in the dressing room of Macy's she switched off the ringer. Now back at home, or rather Chloe's, she unpacked her shopping bags, her cell phone still switched to vibrate.

She owned more than enough clothes and as soon as she felt ready, she'd face Trent and get them. For now the clothes in the bags as well as what she borrowed from Chloe would hold her over. Once she hung up her clothes, she grabbed her phone. She couldn't leave it on vibrate forever. What if her parents or one of her brothers called? She punched in her password. She'd missed six calls, five from Trent and one from her cousin. Her first instinct was to delete all the messages he'd left. Nothing he could say would change her mind. She needed time and space. Her curiosity got the better of her and rather than delete the messages she listened to each one.

On the first message he sounded remorseful as he apologized again and asked her to come back. By the fourth he sounded frustrated. There was no missing the desperation in his voice during the fifth message when he all but begged her to call him back.

All the messages pulled at her heart, turning her water works back on. Even knowing the truth about why he asked her on that first date, she wanted to believe he loved her like he claimed. But how could she believe that from someone who'd started their relationship because of a plan?

After deleting all the messages from Trent she played the last one from Chloe. Her message only asked about how she felt and told Addie to call if she needed anything. Deleting that message as well, she prepared herself some lunch. She'd considered buying something from the mall's food court. When she'd walked into the area though, the smell of greasy burgers, pizza, and Chinese food sent her running for the bathroom. Now though, her stomach grumbled. A can of soup and a cheese sandwich sounded like just the thing.

SEVENTEEN

SHE'D NEVER CONSIDERED herself a chicken. Well, unless it came to thunderstorms, but that was a whole other story. Yet, by Thursday of the following week Addie still hadn't worked up the courage to get her things from Trent's apartment. Which left her with two options, either she sucked it up and went over there or hit the mall and racked up a higher credit card bill. In all honesty, she couldn't decide which option was worse.

So far she'd not spoken with him once. He'd called every day since that dreadful Friday night, leaving her messages when she didn't answer. He'd also stopped by on Monday night, but she'd been up in Worcester meeting with a new client so Chloe had dealt with him. After that unannounced visit she'd feared he'd show up at her office. After all, she did work a few floors below him now. Perhaps because he feared a public scene, he never showed up there. That hadn't stopped him from sending her a dozen roses. Unlike the previous flowers he'd sent, these found their way into the trash, as did the handwritten note attached.

In the end, Addie managed to avoid both solutions. Around noon on Thursday, Chloe made an unexpected visit to her office.

With her shift at the bakery over and her late afternoon class canceled for the day, she'd popped in and invited Addie for lunch.

"I'm not sure eating out is a good idea considering I need a whole new wardrobe. I should work on saving my money where I can." Addie covered her mouth as she yawned again and wondered if another cup of coffee would help. So far today she'd had three cups of coffee and two hot teas, but she still had trouble keeping her eyes open. It had been that way since last week in fact. At first she'd chalked it up to Trent's short business trip. After their falling out on Friday, she'd assumed it was the stress from that. Whatever the cause, she needed her body back to normal. Every morning she got up tired as if she'd not slept at all. The exhaustion only made her nausea worse.

"Do you want me to get your stuff from him?" Chloe asked.

She'd considered asking for Chloe's help but dismissed the idea almost right away. "You'd do that?"

"It makes more sense than buying all new clothes, although I still think you'll move back in with him soon. You love him and I saw the way he acted around you. He loves you, too." Chloe still believed they'd had a simple disagreement, and Addie liked it that way.

Addie considered her cousin's offer. It did make a lot more sense than maxing out her credit card. "You really don't mind?" If she sent him a text message and told him Chloe was coming, she could avoid both seeing and talking to him.

Chloe gave her an exaggerated sigh. "Do you think I would've offered if I minded? If he's around I can go tonight."

She didn't question her cousin again. Instead, she sent Trent a text message. As if he'd had his phone in hand just waiting for a message, he responded answering her question as well as asking if he could call her. When she thanked him for his cooperation, but ignored his question, her phone rang.

"Well, are you going to answer?" Chloe asked. "Whatever you argued about couldn't be that bad."

Answer and get it over with. Maybe he'll stop calling. As the ringtone started over again, she picked up the phone. "Hello."

"God, I'm glad you answered this time."

The sound of his voice brought back one memory after another, each one another stake into her heart. "Don't worry about packing my stuff. Chloe can do it. I'll have her leave my key, too." When she'd rushed out Friday she'd not thought about it.

"Addie, please give me a chance to make things right between us. Come over this weekend so we can talk."

His voice bordered on begging and she wondered if maybe he did care. Just as quickly she wondered if it was all an act. Didn't politicians act in front of the voters all the time? Perhaps this was just another performance for him.

"I can't, Trent, not yet."

"When then?"

The plea in his voice weakened her resolve but she pulled up the image of the documents she'd discovered. "I don't know." She swallowed down the sob that almost escaped her. "Chloe won't take long tonight if you have other plans." Addie hung up before he came back with another plea.

"Are you okay?" Chloe held out a tissue.

With a nod, she accepted it. "I'll be fine." Grabbing her key ring, she yanked Trent's key off. "Most of my stuff is in the master suite and bathroom. But I left my favorite sweatshirt and sneakers in the closet right when you come in."

"Don't worry, I'll get everything." Chloe stuck the key in her jeans pocket and stood. "See you later tonight.

Grateful for her cousin's help, Addie refocused on her work and hoped that would block out the sadness she'd heard in Trent's voice.

THE GENTLEMAN in him said he should pack up Addie's things and make it easy for her cousin. The selfish ass in him decided the longer Chloe stayed at his place, the longer he had to enlist her help. Since the moment Addie walked out on him he'd racked his brain for ways to repair the damage. Thus far, he'd had no success on how he could reach Addie and make her believe him. Maybe once she believed him, she could forgive him. The alternative just wasn't an option. Every time he considered that he might never talk to her or hold her again, his chest ached.

Trent stared out a window, the evening news the only sound in the apartment as he waited for Chloe, who he was still pissed at now that he thought about it. With everything else he'd forgotten about Chloe sending the picture. He didn't believe Chloe had meant any real harm. Still, she'd violated Addie's privacy. Tonight wasn't the time to scold her though. He needed her on his side.

When the security panel buzzed, he told the doorman to send the guest up even before he found out who it was. Eager to speak with Chloe, he opened the apartment door and waited for the elevator.

"Thanks for letting me come by tonight," Chloe said when she stepped off the elevator and saw him. "And before I forget here's your key." She pulled the key from her pocket and held it out.

He hesitated. He didn't want the damn thing back. "Thanks. Come on in." He shoved the key into his own pocket and closed the door. "I think all of Addie's stuff is upstairs. I'll show you."

Chloe didn't speak again as she followed him upstairs, but her expression told him she had a lot on her mind.

"Addie's suitcases are in the closet." He flipped on the

bedroom light and walked halfway into the room. "Do you want my help?"

"Uh, no that's okay," she answered but didn't start packing. "Um, Trent." Chloe shoved her hands into her back jeans pockets. "I don't know what you guys fought about, but I hope it's not me." A guilty expression clouded her face. "I never should've sent that picture in. I'm sorry."

Had Addie not told Chloe the truth? From the sound of it Chloe believed her confession caused their breakup.

"I know you care about my cousin, and she loves you. Is there any way I can help you two work this out? I hate seeing her like this."

He almost laughed. He'd hoped she'd have some ideas. "If you can think of a way, I'm open for suggestions. Just so you know, Chloe, you didn't cause this. I did." Well, maybe her confession had but not in the way she thought. If not for the picture he never would've gotten to know Addie or fallen in love with her. No, all blame for the collapse of their relationship rested on him and Marty.

On the other side of the room, Chloe dropped a suitcase on the bed. "I wish I had some ideas." She grabbed a bunch of skirts from the closet and placed them in the suitcase as he stood by and watched the final remnants of his relationship disappear. "She won't even talk about you. I've never seen her so upset."

It looked like he was back to square one. "I do love her, Chloe." Other than with Addie, he hadn't shared his feeling with anyone. "I just don't know how to fix things." He'd figure it out though, or die trying.

"Have you tried apologizing? Addie has always been a forgiving person. I don't think she's ever held a grudge against anyone."

Obviously, Chloe didn't know how many times he'd tried calling and Addie hadn't answered. "She never takes my calls. I did send her flowers at work."

Chloe looked up from packing. "Really? I didn't see any there. Maybe they didn't make it."

More likely she'd either refused them or tossed them out.

"Maybe she needs a little more time." With the suitcase full, Chloe zipped it up and proceeded to fill the other one.

"I hope you're right." He doubted time would help the situation. "I'll let you finish up. If you need help just ask. And Chloe, when you see Addie please tell her I miss her." He hated using a messenger to convey his feelings, but right now it was all he had. "And tell her I love her."

"Will do."

Trent turned away, but Chloe's voice stopped him. "Trent, I know she loves you. She'll come around."

When he helped Chloe carry the suitcases to her car a little later and watched her drive away, an inexplicable feeling of emptiness took over his body. The only other time he'd experienced something similar had been when his mom died. As terrible as that experience had been at least then he'd had the love and support of the entire Sherbrooke clan behind him. Now, he had no one.

With slow steps he took the stairs from the underground parking garage to the building's main foyer. Once at his private elevator though he changed his mind. Rather than go back upstairs, he turned around and headed for the parking garage again. Right now his place was full of memories and was the last place he wanted to be.

Getting behind the wheel of his Bugatti, he revved the engine, then pulled out, the only destination in mind the open road.

ADDIE'S EYES opened when she heard the front door open and close. How long had she slept? She'd sat down intent on watching her favorite new show, a paranormal drama. Now a popular sitcom played on the television.

"I'm back," Chloe said as she entered the room. "I think I got everything." She dropped down on the couch. "I didn't know you watch this show."

Addie glanced at the screen. "I don't. I fell asleep watching something else and then this started." She turned off the television. She had no interest in the silly show. "Thanks so much for doing that."

"No problem," Chloe answered. "I apologized for the whole picture incident while I was there. I thought maybe that was why you two fought."

She'd not considered that her cousin might blame herself. "It had nothing to do with it."

"That's what he said. He also asked me to tell you he missed you and loves you."

Addie didn't reply. Unless she went into specific details, Chloe would never understand why she doubted his words.

"He looked unhappy, Addie. I think he's sincere. Maybe you two should try talking. Couples fight and disagree all the time. That doesn't mean they can't work out their problems."

She appreciated her cousin's concern, but right now she didn't need her suggestions. "It's complicated, Chloe. Can we just leave it at that for now?"

Chloe's shoulders sagged and she frowned. "If that's what you want. But Addie, if a man told me he loved me and I loved him…" Chloe held up a hand when Addie opened her mouth to speak. "Don't deny it, you love him," she said before she completed her original statement. "Then I'd work things out with him before it was too late."

Under different circumstances she'd take her cousin's advice. Not this time though. "Thanks again for getting my stuff tonight." Addie stood up. "I'm going to bring everything upstairs and unpack. Then go to bed. I'll see you in the morning."

EIGHTEEN

COULD SHE HAVE THE FLU? She'd had it the previous winter and it had knocked her on her butt. She'd spent two full days in bed only getting up for soup and the bathroom. Right now she could easily see herself spending two full days in bed. But when she'd had the flu she'd also had a bunch of other symptoms. She'd had a 101-degree fever for days as well as a cough and sore throat. This time she suffered from none of those things.

Maybe there's some kind of stomach bug going around. *People could get tired from a stomach virus, right?* That would explain her frequent nausea. If that were it, wouldn't she just throw up for twenty-four or forty-eight hours and then be fine? While she'd vomited several times over the past week it wasn't an everyday event. Not to mention she hadn't heard of any stomach bugs going around.

Addie crossed the ideas off her mental list as she sipped her tea the following Thursday. What else could be causing her recent ailments? When she had her monthly period she often got tired and sometimes cranky but not nauseous. Could her body's reaction to that time of the month be changing? People's bodies did change all the time in all kinds of ways. In fact, she had one cousin who had eaten dairy products all her life and now couldn't touch milk without getting sick.

She should be starting her period anytime now. Actually, she'd expected it on Monday, but so far it hadn't started and neither had the horrible cramps she usually suffered from. As if her mind had just put two and two together, she froze. Since going on the pill she'd never missed her period and like clock-work they started on Monday. Here it was Thursday and nothing, not even a single cramp.

No, she couldn't be pregnant. Sure, she and Trent had stopped using condoms because she was on the pill, but those things were great at preventing pregnancy. Yes, the doctor said they didn't prevent pregnancies one hundred percent of the time, but she'd never had a friend use the pill and get pregnant. Yet if the doctors said it was even a remote possibility then she guessed it was.

Panic like she'd never experienced before welled up in her chest and she took a gulp of her tea. There had to be another explanation. Stress maybe, didn't that do all kinds of crazy things to your body? Addie latched onto the explanation. *I've had plenty of stress in life before and never felt this way,* her mind whispered dashing her hopes.

She went for another sip of her tea only then realizing she'd finished it. Covering her eyes with her hand she sat still. *Only one way to find out.* Addie pushed back her office chair. Then after a brief stop at Tara's desk, she left for the closest pharmacy.

Not even an hour later, Addie stood in the private bathroom off her office and placed the pregnancy test stick next to the other two and held her breath as she waited. In less than a minute the tiny positive blue sign appeared just as it had done in the first two tests from the three-pack kit she'd bought.

Around her, the room spun and she grabbed onto the sink counter. No, there had to be a mistake. She took her pill every morning with breakfast. She never missed one. Wasn't that how women became pregnant while on the pill, by skipping doses? Once the room stopped moving, she sat down on the toilet seat cover. Maybe the tests were faulty. Maybe she bought a defective box. "I'll buy another box and that one will work fine." Addie jumped up, grabbed her purse and headed back out.

Deciding that the first pharmacy must sell defective products, she headed for the pharmacy located in the Providence Place Mall. When she dropped her purchase on the counter, the cashier gave her a curious look, but she understood why. After all she was buying four pregnancies tests, all from different manufacturers. If she'd been working at the register and someone came up with that many, she'd probably give them a strange look as well.

"One of these has to work right," she muttered as she entered her office later. Once in the privacy of her bathroom, she opened up all the individual boxes and prayed for a different result.

HE DECIDED to give her a little time. Calling her and leaving messages every day hadn't helped. His flowers hadn't helped and neither had the message he'd given her cousin. Perhaps some time to think would. Right now he figured it couldn't hurt anything.

"Mr. Sherbrook, Marty Phillips is here to see you," Shirley said from the doorway.

Trent almost told Shirley to reschedule the meeting. He knew if Marty questioned him about Addie he'd lose it on the guy. So far, both Marty and the media knew nothing about their breakup. He hoped it would stay that way. "Send him in, Shirley."

Shirley disappeared and Marty entered with a smile on his face. "Have you seen today's *Providence Gazette*?"

Wasn't it a similar line that had gotten him into this mess? "No, not yet," he answered with suspicion. Judging by Marty's smile it wasn't bad news, but when it came to the media you never knew.

"The paper did an election poll which included you, Potter and Runnel." Marty took a newspaper from his briefcase and handed it to Trent. "At least according to the poll voters are most likely to vote for you, although Potter isn't far behind."

Trent looked at the poll results. According to it, fifty percent of the people asked said they'd vote for him in the election while forty said they'd vote for Potter. Although the election was still a while away, the number should thrill him. Instead, a knot formed in his stomach. They'd used Addie to achieve this. He didn't doubt for a minute that his recent relationship with her had changed the way people saw him.

"I also heard that the Belands were quite taken with you and Addie at the auction. If you and Addie attend a few more of the same functions and develop a strong relationship, you'll have Vincent in your corner. Maybe invite him for a round of golf, too. He's an avid golfer. Consider making a contribution to the hospital as well."

He nodded. He had every intention of winning Addie back and until then he didn't want to discuss her with Marty.

Satisfied with Trent's response, Marty continued. "It's still too soon to start campaign ads, but we want to get things in motion. I've already contacted, Ben Astor; he did a lot of work on your uncle's ads. I'm waiting to hear back from his office so we can all sit down and talk."

Trent added little to the conversation as Marty went over the meeting's agenda. So far things looked right on track and Marty appeared confident he would soon find himself a Senator in Washington. Two weeks earlier the meeting would've left him on cloud nine. Now it left him wishing he could turn the clock back. If he could do that he'd ask Addie out the day he'd bumped into her, long before Marty's crazy plan.

"Will we be reading about an engagement anytime soon?" Marty asked touching on his relationship for the first time.

Trent thought back to his proposal. The whole night had played out much differently than he'd planned it. "I don't know. I'll let you know."

"At least she quit the bakery," Marty said as a knock sounded at the door.

Thankful for the interruption, Trent told Shirley to enter.

"I'm sorry to interrupt, but your cousin Jake is here to see you."

As much as he'd rather have Jake on the other side of conference table instead of Marty, he realized they still had matters to discuss. "Can you please tell him, I'll be here a while and to just meet me at my place. Paul will know to let him in."

Shirley nodded and closed the door.

"I HELPED MYSELF. I didn't think you'd mind," Jake said, a beer in his hand when Trent entered his kitchen a few hours later.

A cold beer sounded perfect right now to him as well. "I think I'll grab one myself." Trent left his briefcase on a chair. As he headed for the refrigerator, he unknotted his tie, eager to lose the thing.

"I thought Addie would be here before you. She moved in with you, didn't she?" Jake tipped back his beer bottle and took a long swig.

Trent used more force than necessary on the bottle cover and it flew across the counter before it hit the wall. "She moved out last week." He ignored the discarded cover and took a gulp from his bottle.

"What did you do?" Jake asked with no hesitation. "Don't

deny it. I know you. If she moved out you must have screwed something up."

Trent didn't deny his cousin's allegations. "That would be putting it mildly." Before Jake could question him again, he went on and changed the subject. "Where's Charlie?"

"Atlanta at a medical symposium until Wednesday. I thought I'd visit you for a few days and then go see my nephew." Jake worked at pulling the label off his beer bottle. "So what did you do that made Addie leave?"

So far he'd come up with no ways for winning her back and her cousin hadn't had any ideas. Maybe Jake would have some suggestions. "I used her." He took another swig of beer to moisten his dry mouth. Then Trent shared everything with Jake from how they first met to how she'd discovered the binders in his desk. As he shared the information, it again struck him just how cold and heartless he'd been.

Across the table Jake shook his head, his mouth in a tight grim line. "Christ, Trent, what were you thinking? I'm surprised she didn't hit you when she found out."

Her walking out of his life hurt more than any physical punch ever would.

"Sara said she warned you about Marty. Too bad you didn't listen."

He'd forgotten all about his conversation with Sara and her warning about Marty. He wondered what Marty had done in the past. "Right now that's a moot point." Maybe someday he'd make inquiries; for now he had more important matters. "I've tried everything I can think of, but she wants nothing to do with me. I don't suppose you have any useful ideas on how I can fix this mess."

Jake studied him. "Do you love her or do you want her back because of the election?"

"You have to ask? I brought her to Callie and Dylan's. I had her move in with me. Hell, the night she walked out I proposed."

His cousin's doubts about his intentions cut him deep. Jake more than anyone else should know him better.

"I figured as much, but I wanted to check." Jake fell silent again as if deep in thought. "If I were in her place, it'd take a hell of a lot more than flowers and an apology to give you another chance, so you need to think big. Even then, I wouldn't blame her if she said forget it and moved on, especially given your reputation."

Although Jake only voiced the thought he'd had himself, the urge to punch his cousin took root. "Thanks a lot," he said his voice dripping with sarcasm.

Trent's sarcasm didn't seem to bother Jake. "Come on, Trent. Put yourself in her shoes and then think about it."

Even if he agreed with his cousin, he had no intention of admitting it. "Something big? As in expensive big?" If it would help, he'd buy her the most expensive gift he could find.

Jake walked away as he shook his head. "That's not what I meant." He pulled another beer from the refrigerator. "Want another?"

Trent nodded. He'd more or less known his cousin wasn't referring to a big expensive gift. That would be too easy. "I need to make a big emotional gesture, right?" He said even though he already knew the answer.

He must have made a pained expression because Jake laughed at him as he handed him his beer. "You screwed up big time. Did you think a simple solution would magically appear? You need to prove to her that you love her. That you would give up anything for her. You need to shed some blood in order to fix this one."

At the moment he wanted to shed some of his cousin's blood. "How did you patch things up with Charlie when she left you?" Although now married and very happy by the looks of it, Charlie had broken up with Jake a few months into their relationship.

"Believe it or not that wasn't my fault. Actually it wasn't either of our faults. Rather it was misunderstanding. She misinterpreted something she saw and jumped to the wrong conclusion. After a while she figured that out and came to me."

Trent guessed Jake gave him the condensed version of events because Charlie didn't strike him as the type to jump to conclusions.

"Going by what you told me, Addie didn't misunderstand anything and every one of her reactions was justified."

Trent put down his bottle of beer. "I need something stronger tonight." Between his meeting with Marty and now his conversation with Jake, he needed something that would help him forget for a little while. A few shots of his favorite cognac would accomplish the job.

As he hoped, three extra large shots of cognac combined with the beer relaxed him enough that for the first time since Addie left his thoughts didn't remain fixed on her. In fact, the only thing on his mind was his bed. So not long after he finished his third drink, he left Jake watching television and headed upstairs. He'd managed to stay awake long enough to strip off his shoes and shirt before he fell into his cold empty bed. Thanks to the cognac, however, Addie's absence on her side of the bed didn't register, and within minutes he was asleep.

Unfortunately, he didn't stay asleep. Whenever he drank more than he should he fell asleep as soon as his head hit the pillow, but he never managed to stay asleep. He assumed it had something to do with how the alcohol affected the brain because it always happened and tonight was no different.

The clock on the nightstand read two, and Trent stared at the ceiling wide awake. With the effects of the alcohol gone, his brain registered the empty space where Addie should be. As he examined the ceiling, he thought back to his conversation with Jake. He needed to make a grand gesture. Proposing would be considered such an act, but he couldn't do that. Even if she hadn't already said no, she'd take it as part of his plan for fixing his image. No, it had to be something else. But what? Damn, he wished he could just buy her a gift and win her back that way. He could come up with half a dozen gifts without even putting any thought into it. He knew that method would never work with Addie.

Come on Sherbrooke, you're intelligent. Think of something. Maybe if he focused on what his gesture must accomplish that would help. Whatever he did must prove that he loved her for her, not because she made him look like a decent guy. It also had to prove she came before everything else, including his political career. Slowly an idea formed. By the time the clock numbers read three, he believed he had it. Now he needed to see her. What he had in mind couldn't be expressed in a text message or over the phone. Considering the fact she never returned his phone calls, getting a one-on-one meeting might prove impossible.

Turning onto his side, Trent punched his pillow. Today he'd try calling again. If she didn't answer he'd stop by her house. It may take more than one trip, but eventually she'd let him in if for no other reason than to tell him to stop bothering her. Once they were in the same room he'd put his heart on the table and hope for the best.

AFTER THANKING HER FRIEND LYDIA, a friend from high school who worked as a nurse at Rhode Island hospital, Addie hung up the phone. That's what she got for not reading the information sheet included with her prescription. Never had she heard that antibiotics could reduce the effectiveness of birth control pills, and when her doctor wrote the prescription for her strep throat, she hadn't mentioned it. According to Lydia though, her prescription should've have come with a fact sheet listing the side effects. Although the sheets contained important information, Addie always tossed them without even glancing at them. She'd never had a problem until now. And what a problem she had.

Learning of Trent's deception had crushed her heart, but at least she'd assumed she'd never have to see him again. A baby would make that impossible. Or would it? If she never saw him, he'd never know about the baby. In an ideal world all children would have two parents who loved them, but plenty of children were raised by single parents. Her baby wouldn't lack for love either, even if Trent were not around. Her parents might be disappointed when they first found out about the baby and no marriage, but they would get over it and spoil their grandson or granddaughter. Then of course there were her brothers. Her baby would have four loving and protective uncles. Although there would be the possibility they'd be loving uncles from behind bars after they killed Trent for getting her pregnant.

Addie let the idea of not telling Trent simmer and soon her conscience came online. The memory of Trent holding James in Connecticut formed, and their conversation from the garden replayed. For all his faults, Trent would be a good father. Plus, he'd be able to give their child so much more than she ever could. If she kept the baby a secret, not only would she be depriving Trent, but also their child.

Addie dropped her head in her hands. If she told him, Trent would always be involved in her life. A constant reminder of their relationship and how he'd used her. When he did marry, she'd have to see him with some beautiful wife on his arm. She'd likely see him with more children as well. How could she ever handle that? Just the mere thought made the tears flow.

It'll get better. It won't always hurt this much even if he does have a beautiful woman on his arm. She wiped away the tears from her face and eyed her cell phone. She had to tell him. Her emotions didn't matter, telling him was the right thing. With a sniffle, she checked her watch. Outside, the sun had disappeared and now only the moon and stars filled the sky, but even so it couldn't be that late.

Ten o'clock—no that couldn't be right. Addie grabbed her phone. Sure enough the phone read ten o'clock. *So much for calling and asking to see him tonight.* Her news would have to wait one more day.

NINETEEN

"DAMN IT, Trent. I wish I'd never come up." Jake wiped the blood from his lip. "Last night you got drunk and passed out. Now this."

Trent rested his forearms on his knees as his cousin took care of his bloody lip. "You agreed to practice with me. It's not my fault your ground fighting sucks." They'd both taken up boxing and ground fighting in boarding school. Trent still practiced regularly with a personal coach, but he didn't know about his cousin.

"I only agreed because I thought it might improve your mood. You've been an ass all day."

He had no smart reply for that. Even he recognized his foul mood, which had set in after he called Addie and got her voice mail yet again. As the day wore on and no return call came his mood digressed further. Hoping that some physical activity would distract him, he'd asked Jake to spar. So far the exercise had only gained him a sore jaw from Jake's elbow. On the plus side, though, it had killed some time and given his cousin a bloody lip.

"The split lip improves your appearance."

Jake wiped his bloody fingers on his T-shirt. "Give me a minute and I'll improve yours, too."

"You can try."

With no warning, Jake lunged at him, taking Trent down. The two men struggled for the upper hand, neither willing to concede until the cell phone rang.

"That's yours not mine," Jake panted, as the ring continued.

Trent jumped up and sprinted across the gym for his cell phone. *Finally.* Addie's name and number filled the screen. "Addie," he said a little out of breath himself.

At first only silence came though the phone. "Hi, Trent. I can call you back if this is a bad time."

"No, it's fine." He tried to get his breathing more normal. "I'm glad you called."

Silence again greeted his ear.

"If you're home, can I come over? We need to talk." Reluctance filled her voice, but he ignored it. She'd called and wanted to see him. That was all that mattered.

"Come on over anytime. I'm home."

Still seated on the floor, Jake listened and gave him a thumbs up when Trent told Addie to come over.

"I'm at the office so I should be there in about five minutes."

Shit. That didn't give him much time to clean up, but he couldn't see her like this. Sweat covered him and he smelled about as good as a dirty gym sock, not to mention he hadn't shaved. "Okay, see you then." He ended the call, and then looked at his cousin. "Jake, when Addie gets here, let her in. I need a shower." He didn't wait for a reply. Right now time wasn't on his side.

ADDIE STEPPED off the elevator but made it no further. She'd spent the night before and early morning preparing what she'd say. A client appointment in the afternoon distracted her from the task ahead, but now her mind swirled again as her insides practiced the jitterbug. How would he react? An illegitimate child with a woman couldn't be good for his precious new image. Although, if he became the doting father it might redeem him in the eyes of many voters. After all, this wasn't the nineteenth century. People did have children all the time without getting married.

With that, another thought popped into her head and sent ice through her veins. What if Trent demanded sole custody? These days most judges awarded joint custody except in extreme circumstances, but who knew? He could argue that he had the resources to raise a child while Addie didn't. Trent also had money and connections; he could use both and sway a judge in his direction.

Maybe she shouldn't tell him. What were the chances she could avoid seeing him over the next nine months or so? Her office was only floors below his. More than likely, they'd bump into each other at some point. If he saw her tomorrow he'd never suspect anything, but what if he saw her in seven months. He'd notice then.

"It's the right thing," she whispered for the hundredth time. Crossing the floor, she got the impression this was how prisoners during the French revolution felt walking to the Guillotine.

The door opened only moments after she rang the bell, but not by the Sherbrooke she wanted. "Addie, come on in," Jake said. He stood in the doorway, his face sweat stained and blood on the shirt he wore.

Addie hesitated, and then stepped forward. "Is Trent home?" She clasped her hands behind her.

"You mean Grumpy? Yeah, he's in the shower."

For the moment the purpose of her visit faded. "Grumpy?"

"Yeah, you know like the dwarf from *Snow White*. He's

about as pleasant as that." Jake paused then shook his head. "No, I'm wrong. He's worse."

Great, Trent in a bad mood. Who knew how a grumpy Trent would take the news? "If he's in a bad mood maybe I should come back later."

"And have him split my lip again?" He pointed to his bottom lip, which looked swollen. "Unless you don't care for my well-being, I suggest you stay."

Addie cracked a smile despite the seriousness of her visit. Jake had a knack for making people laugh. She'd noticed that in Connecticut as well. "I guess I'll stay then." Behind her back she tightened her grip. "You two were fighting?"

Jake took her by the elbow and led her further inside. "I thought it would improve his mood. This was all it did." He gestured toward his mouth again as he sat.

Since it appeared appropriate, she followed suit and took the armchair across from him. At first neither spoke, instead Jake studied her.

"I've never seen him like this," he said, breaking the silence. "This situation with you is tearing him up."

Yeah, because his plan went down the drain. "I doubt that."

"I've known my cousin a lot longer than you and this isn't him. He loves you," Jake said his voice a mix of kindness and authority.

"Did he tell you why I left?" Maybe he didn't know the truth about her and Trent's relationship.

Jake crossed his arms and leaned back, disgust on his face. "Yeah, he told me everything. What can I say? My cousin can be an ass at times. *But,* he loves you. His proposal had nothing to do with any plan."

If she could only believe Jake, but how could she? Wouldn't Trent's cousin say anything in his defense? "I know you believe that—"

"But you don't," Jake interrupted her. "I get it. At least think about it and hear what he has to say. Despite his flaws he's a good guy."

"Addie," Trent said.

She looked toward the stairs as he came down. Dressed in jeans and a T-shirt, his hair looked damp and he'd not bothered with any shoes. Right away, the sight brought tears and she prayed she could hold them back long enough to say what she'd come for.

"I'm sorry I kept you waiting." He stopped near the coffee table but made no move to touch her.

"It's okay. I haven't been here long." Up close she noticed the nicks on his face from shaving and the dark circles under his eyes.

"That's my cue." Jake stood and, without another word, left.

In her lap, she squeezed her fingers. "I'm sorry. I didn't think that you might have company."

Trent pointed his thumb toward the stairs. "He's more of an annoyance. I'd rather see you. Actually, I planned to stop by your house tonight."

She offered him a weak smile. "I guess this saves you a trip." She cleared her throat. "Trent, I have something important to tell you." She'd known this would be difficult but not this bad.

"So do I." He sat down on the coffee table his knees mere inches from hers. "Do you mind if I go first?"

Addie shook her head. If she opened her mouth now she feared the dam holding back her tears would burst.

"You already know about Marty's plan. I wish it wasn't true but it is. There's nothing I can do about the past." He took both her hands in his. "But Addie from the very first time we met, you intrigued me. You wouldn't even let me buy you a new coffee after I spilled yours even though you recognized me."

His words brought back their first encounter and her chest tightened.

"That's why I sat down that day. I'd been thinking about you and suddenly there you were. From the very start I thought of you as a woman I enjoyed spending time with. I never saw you as some pawn in a plan." Trent paused and swallowed. "Then before I knew it, I was in love with you."

Trent's thick and unsteady voice pulled at her and tears slid down her face.

"When I asked you to marry me, it was because I love you, not because Marty says I need a wife." He released her hands and wiped a tear from her cheek. "This time without you has been unbearable. I need you, Addison." His voice cracked and his eyes glistened with tears.

Could she believe him? More than anything she wanted to. What if this was all just an act? "Trent, how do I know this isn't just ploy? A way to get me to fall in line with your plan? I love you and want to believe you, but I just don't know if I can." She spoke with as reasonable a voice as she could manage.

He wiped another tear away, and then took her hands again in his. "I know. That's why I've decided not to run for the Senate. Marty let all the media outlets know at four o'clock this morning that I have no intention of running. It was on the front page of all the papers and on the morning news. Someone else can have Senator Harrison's seat."

Addie's mouth dropped open. "What?"

"You're more important than some seat in Senate. If it means you'll marry me, I won't ever go into politics. I'll stay with Sherbrooke Enterprises for the rest of my life. Or come and work for you. Hell, if it makes you happy I'll be a stay at home dad when we have children."

Her mind reeled from his words. "You won't ever run for office?" Her voice came out as a mere whisper.

"I'll never enter politics if that's what you want," he said repeating his previous statement.

Her mind worked on processing his words. "But it's important to you, Trent."

He raised their joined hands toward his mouth and kissed her knuckles. "You're more important. Please say you'll marry me." Trent released her hands then pulled out the diamond engagement ring he'd proposed with before.

PLEASE ANSWER ME. Addie sat across from him staring at the ring. He'd said what was in his heart and she'd at least listened. But had it been enough? So far she'd said little. "Addie, do you need time?" It would kill him if she left tonight without answering him, but he'd give her more time and space if she needed it.

Addie met his eyes, tears falling down her cheeks. "No, I don't need time," she said in a broken whisper. "I can't let you give up your goals. If you don't run someday, you'll regret it and blame me. You'll resent me."

She hadn't said no. That was a start. "That's not—"

"I need a promise from you," she said before he could finish.

"Anything."

"Promise you'll stick with your plan and run someday, maybe in six years."

"But Addie—"

"Promise me. I know how important it is to you." Her voice left no room for argument.

He pulled her left hand toward him. "If that's what you want." He slipped the ring on her finger. "Now, will you marry me?" *She'll say yes.* He repeated the sentence over and over in his head. She'd marry him.

Her eyes dropped from his face and locked on the diamond. As if making sure it was real she touched it and then looked up. Tears still welled up in her eyes, but a brilliant smile lit up her face. She nodded and sniffled at the same time. "Yes." She threw her arms around his neck.

The weight he'd carried around since she left lifted from his body and he wrapped his arms around her. Then he captured her mouth, the feel of her lips against his sending a shock wave through his whole body. "I love you," he whispered against her mouth.

Addie kissed him back, her lips barely touching his. "I love you, too." She pulled back and looked at him. "I need to tell you something."

The excitement from before faded from her voice, and he recalled the original reason for her visit. "I'm listening." He took her hand again, the need for physical contact great.

"Trent, I'm... " Addie stopped. "I'm pregnant, Trent."

Blood pounded in his ears and he stared at Addie.

"Trent?"

"How? Are you sure?" She'd told him she was on the pill.

"Do you remember when I had strep?"

Trent nodded as giddiness built up inside him.

"I guess antibiotics and the pill don't mix well. And yeah, I'm sure. I haven't seen a doctor yet, but I took seven pregnancy tests and they all came back positive."

"Pregnant." He pictured himself holding his own son or daughter. "Seven tests!"

"Are you mad?" she asked with caution.

"Mad?" How could she think he was mad? "I'm euphoric. I've got you and soon I'll have a son or daughter. I couldn't be happier."

Trent stood, pulling her up with him, and crushed her against his chest. "I do think we should get married sooner rather than later now." He kissed her before she answered.

When they broke apart her face again beamed with joy. "How about we start making plans later tonight. Right now I have something else in mind." She grabbed his hand and tugged him toward the stairs.

"I love the way you think."

. . .

THE END

DO YOU WANT MORE SHERBROOKES? Read on for an excerpt from Gray's story, More Than A Billionaire (http://www.christinatetreault.com/books/more-than-a-billionaire/)

Made in the USA
Middletown, DE
17 June 2022